Helen FitzGerald is one of thirteen children and grew up in Victoria. Australia. She now lives in Glasgow with her husband and two children. Helen has worked as a parole officer and social worker for over ten years. *Dead Lovely* is her first novel.

DEAD LOVELY

Krissie and Sarah have been best friends since they were children. While Sarah has been married to Kyle since university, trying — unsuccessfully — to have a baby, Krissie is carefree and single . . . But then Krissie accidentally becomes pregnant following a dalliance in a Tenerife toilet cubicle. For Sarah, who's long been trying to conceive, Krissie's unplanned pregnancy seems unfair. Things between them get worse during a walking holiday round Loch Lomond with Kyle. At first the days pass blissfully as the three friends laugh, chat and reminisce. But one night friendship turns to betrayal, and betrayal turns to murder . . .

HELEN FITZGERALD

DEAD LOVELY

Complete and Unabridged

ULVERSCROFT
Leicester

First published in Great Britain in 2008 by
Faber and Faber Limited
London

First Large Print Edition
published 2009
by arrangement with
Faber and Faber
London

British Library CIP Data

FitzGerald, Helen., 1966 –
Dead lovely
1. Female friendship- -Fiction. 2. Childlessness- -Fiction.
3. Jealousy- -Fiction. 4. Vacations- -Scotland- -Loch
Lomond and the Trossachs National Park- -Fiction.
5. Murder- -Fiction. 6. Large type books.
I. Title
823.9′2–dc22

ISBN 978–1–84782–626–8

Published by
F. A. Thorpe (Publishing)
Anstey, Leicestershire

Set by Words & Graphics Ltd.
Anstey, Leicestershire
Printed and bound in Great Britain by
T. J. International Ltd., Padstow, Cornwall

This book is printed on acid-free paper

Acknowledgements

This book wouldn't have happened without the faith and perseverance of my agent, Adrian Weston at Raft PR: thank you, thank you.

Louise Thurtell, Lauren Finger and everyone at Allen & Unwin — thanks for turning this into something I'm truly proud of.

Thanks to Wanda Gloude at Ambo Anthos, who was the first to believe in the book, and to Helen Francis at Faber & Faber.

And to the tireless Sergio Casci who keeps me sane and very, very happy.

1

Some people find themselves all at once, like an explosion. Backpacking in the Himalayas maybe, or tripping on acid. Some people study the art of finding themselves, and graduate — or not — after years of diligence. I found myself bit by bit, through a series of accidents really.

The first bit I found was in a tent on the West Highland Way. My best friend Sarah was asleep. Her husband was lying beside her, and I was swallowing his semen.

I discovered the next piece of me at the bottom of a cliff, where I dragged Sarah's dead body, bumping her head from rock to rock. Sarah, my best friend since we were little girls, who I'd betrayed and murdered.

And then, in the darkness of my parents' attic, I found the rest of me.

★ ★ ★

Until a week ago I had only made one really significant mistake in my life. I knew I had faults. Little things, like I was vain and impatient and I drank twenty units of alcohol a week, which is a lie, because it had to be at least twenty-five, which is also a lie. But I had only done one thing that I was truly ashamed of.

I'd gone to Tenerife with Marj from work, who knew a guy who knew a guy who could get us some pills. So Marj and I spent seven days sleeping on black sand drinking orange juice, and seven nights in a nightclub touching each other's faces and dancing to specks on the dance floor, which seemed somehow beautiful and threatening at the same time. I was dancing to one particular speck one evening when I realised a man with white teeth, dressed in a khaki T-shirt and Diesel jeans, was dancing with me and also understanding the speck on the floor.

We looked at each other for a moment, and smiled, both thinking exactly the same thing at the same time. 'At last, someone who knows me.'

I shook my head in disbelief. I'd found him!

He touched my shoulder with love, with a true touch of love. I felt his face with my warm fingers. Then I took his hand, walked calmly to the ladies' toilets, pushed him into the cubicle, curled my black thong down my legs, and pushed his head down and into me. He surfaced with surprising swiftness, and we made love against the pure white tiled wall of that wonderful, soft place. We looked into each other's eyes, held hands, and made love.

It's weird how a hangover creeps up on you. Mine came at the same time as the man with the teeth did. Almost like a gunshot, exhaustion, eye pain and bad breath banged into me. Boom. I was hungover, and I could see that the white grit between the tiles was actually grey with the settled, damp fumes of pee; that the toilet was brown with steamed-on shit; and that my man, my beautiful true love, had a piece of something orange fused between his two front teeth.

I wished he would wipe the slime from me off his face, and I needed a drink of water.

I found Marj and hauled her from her place on the dance floor and we went back to our hotel room.

Until a week ago, that was the only big mistake I had ever made. The only thing I truly regretted. Conceiving little Robbie in that way. My little baby, Robbie.

2

It was Sarah who helped me through the pregnancy. We had a history friendship — time had earned us the right to each other's unconditional love. And while we annoyed each other endlessly, especially as the years morphed us into our mothers, we felt true love for each other. If the parking inspector did not back down, it was Sarah I rang for a whinge. If I had an ingrown hair that required surgery, it was Sarah, the nurse, who operated. If I needed to sit on a sofa and not talk, it was Sarah who silently provided the very good crisps. She was my rock, my protector.

Sarah and I met when we were four, and I immediately loved her because she was pretty, with well-brushed shiny blonde hair and bright blue doll-like eyes. She was never alone in the playground, was never worried about people liking her or not, and was soothing to look at, like the sea.

Sarah was everything I wasn't. She was sensible, and would never rollerskate down a steep hill or spill juice on her spelling jotter. She was girly. While Santa brought me water pistols and gardening rakes, Sarah got pink fluffy things and dolls that peed and cried (and freaked me out). But perhaps the biggest difference between us was that Sarah was an indoors person. She could spend all day in her room playing with Tiny Tears — cooking for her in her mini kitchen, ironing for her with a mini iron, dressing her in those mini dresses.

I, on the other hand, hated being indoors. I'd play in the street, in Pollok Park, at the arcade, in my friends' gardens, but when I played at Sarah's house we almost always stayed inside. If I ever managed to get Sarah to come outside to play when we were little, it would be on the strict condition that Tiny Tears could come too, and while I would build a mini tree house for the doll to escape to, Sarah would feed her porridge, wipe her face, change her nappy and rock her to sleep.

* * *

Poor Sarah. A baby was all she'd ever really wanted for as long as I could remember. At first when Sarah was trying to conceive she'd ring her husband Kyle excitedly at his surgery and get him to come home and do it because the time was right — her discharge was clear, her temperature was high, and she was horny

5

as all hell. Afterwards they'd giggle as he put his stethoscope on her tummy to 'listen to him swim'.

But as time passed, Kyle found he couldn't leave patients waiting, or he had home visits to do, and Sarah wondered if her cycle was more elusive than she'd believed. After a while, she decided that it wandered around the month invisibly, and in order to catch it she and Kyle should have sex every night.

This went on for two years. They got good at it. Who needs lubrication? One difficult shove at the beginning is a small price to pay for efficiency.

But after twenty-four months of nightly sex, the sperm still seemed to be doing bugger all.

So Sarah left work, deciding the stress in Intensive Care could be having a detrimental effect on her ovaries. Then Kyle used his clout as the longest-serving GP in South Shawlands Surgery to get a speedy referral to the best fertility specialist in the United Kingdom. Sarah took medication, felt ill and grumpy, no longer tended her garden with gentle care, put the renovation plans for the weekender near Loch Katrine on hold and moaned to her oldest and closest friend — me — every night on the telephone.

'Kyle is working all the time! Why? Why? Why?'

The first time she rang, I suggested we go out and get drunk.

'Do you want the baby to grow up short?' exclaimed Sarah.

Next I suggested going out for dinner. I only suggested this once, after she put me off mussels marinara forever with her concern about bacteria.

I am deeply ashamed of this now, but after months and months of calls I got tired of it all. I had listened and counselled with proper concern for so long. I had cried with her, my friend whose inexplicable maternal urge had exploded inside her with enthusiasm but without capacity. I had bought her homeopathic remedies, books, nicotine patches, gum and inhalers. What about this? That? Get Kyle checked out. Check your elasticity down there. Clear and elastic. Most important, relax.

But none of it had worked, and I got tired.

So, there came a time when I found myself taking a very deep breath before answering the late-night calls. There would be a silence and a snuffle, and I would ask her how she was and the answer would never be good. She was obsessed. Everything in her world had found its way to her ovaries. Dinner, work, clothing, footwear and dog shit were ovary-related.

In turn, the single aim of my conversations became ovary-evasion. 'How's the stone wall going in Loch Katrine?' I asked her once at 10.33 p.m. on a weeknight.

'I've stopped,' she said. 'The strain might be bad for my ovaries.'

★　★　★

When Sarah rang at 11.03 p.m. one night to say Kyle didn't even want to do it anymore, I'm afraid I snapped and told her to pull herself together. I told her that not having sex was probably quite a significant factor in not getting pregnant, and unless she sorted herself out who could blame Kyle for not wanting to go anywhere near her?

She hung up on me.

Ashamed at my outburst, I phoned back. She didn't answer. I phoned back again. And at last I got Kyle, who said in a conspiratorial voice, 'She's not available.'

So I went round and knocked on the door. Kyle answered with that annoying expression of his. I remembered that expression from university days when I'd shared a flat with Kyle and a friend of ours, Chas.

I'd met Chas while eating dhal with my

right hand in Goa. He was living in a tree at the time, as you do, and pondering. He was cute, and we had our Scottish background in common, but he was not my type. He was kind of grungy: scraggly, rough around the edges, a bit too skinny, but with magical eyes that someone one day would fall hopelessly in love with. He wore unusual clothes that he threw together oddly, and looked better naked than clothed. I knew this because I had seen him in an outdoor shower once in Goa and he was surprisingly muscular and square, not at all weedy. I found his company to be the most comfortable I had ever had. No expectations, no bothersome political differences, and no sexual tensions. Chas always said yes if I needed an emergency date to make an ex-boyfriend jealous, but I never once considered him as a sexual partner, never thought of him in that way at all. There was one time when we got very drunk at a medical ball and he tried to kiss me in the taxi on the way home. It felt like I was kissing my brother and I pushed him away with a 'Yuck!' We'd both laughed, but it had felt kind of weird.

Chas moved into my flat a while later and spent his time singing and occasionally proclaiming truths about beauty, among other things. We'd get openly annoyed with each other when the milk or the loo roll ran out, and read the papers over breakfast in companionable silence.

Kyle was mostly fun to live with. He could whistle the theme tune to every seventies cop show, and not just the obvious ones like *Kojak* or *The Sweeney*. We're talking *Rookies*, *SWAT* and *Barnaby Jones*. But when he had an exam and Chas and I were making too much noise in the lounge he'd come in and sit on the sofa, his facial features settling around his nose, all scrunched up in a tight ball of bloodless tension. We'd get the hint pretty quickly and go to bed so he could study.

Kyle was the only one in the flat who really had to get through a lot of work at university. I was doing social work and never had to study very hard. And Chas dropped out of medicine after a year, threw himself into ill temper, and started smoking copious amounts of dope with the apparent long-term plan of graduating from depression to schizophrenia.

I looked at Kyle all these years later and thought to myself, why can't you just say how you feel? 'My wife is driving me crazy and I wish you hadn't upset her.' Instead, he stood there as he always had when distressed, fizzing inside with a tornado of emotions that he had no idea how to harness.

He beckoned me into the kitchen and there was an awkward moment as we stood trying to chat as if nothing was going down.

'How's work?' he asked me.

'Busy! Awful!' I replied.

It struck me as we stood there talking that it was probably the first time Kyle and I had been alone since he'd met Sarah.

We were all twenty-one when the two of them met. Sarah had dropped around to see me after work one day and Kyle answered the door. He'd just had a shower, so he had no top on. Chas and I felt the sexual tension between them straight away so we made our excuses and went to the pub, feeling giggly and excited at the prospect of our two friends getting together.

Later that night, and throughout the courtship that followed, our respective mates gave us glorious details that we exchanged and analysed.

According to Sarah, on that first evening they had four coffees and talked for three hours about hospitals.

According to Kyle, Sarah leant forward, affording him a clear view of her bosom.

According to Sarah, Kyle was everything she'd ever wanted — a decent, hard-working, honest man.

According to Kyle, Sarah was the most beautiful woman he'd ever seen.

Sarah loved how Kyle was so patient and respectful.

Kyle said by the time Sarah agreed to do it he'd developed wanker's cramp.

Kyle's proposal was everything Sarah had ever dreamt of . . .

And the ring cost a fucking fortune.

Sarah looked sensational as a bride. Her hair was as curly, blonde and glossy as it had been when she was tiny and her whole face beamed with happiness. Kyle couldn't take his eyes off her. The perfect wedding for the perfect couple. The wedding party was a sea of large hats, kilts and stiff two-piece skirt-suits. I wore a shiny mauve dress and felt like a Teletubby. Sarah's mum mustered her acting skills to evoke emotion in the university chapel with a Shakespearean sonnet. Kyle's best friend, Derek, read out a raucously sexual speech.

'Sarah will make the perfect doctor's wife,' he said. 'Big, y'know, ideas, and a goer, according to the residents in the Royal! But, seriously,' he said to a half-silent, half-chortling audience, 'seriously, though, they do make a wonderful couple . . . and she does go like a bunny.'

Sarah's dad, who she hadn't seen for years,

drank too much and groped several guests on the dance floor.

After the honeymoon they sold Sarah's Southside flat and bought a three-bedroom tenement in the trendy West End, which Sarah did up. Two years later they sold the flat for an extortionate sum, bought a four-bedroom house a little further out ('where the good schools are'), and started trying to make babies.

Unable to control her reproductive system, Sarah concentrated on the things she could control. From the outside, it seemed as though Sarah was renovating her husband at the same time as she was renovating the house, redressing old windows with carefully selected fabric, feminising bed linen and bathroom accessories, ripping out kitchens and cheap lean-tos, and re-roofing, bit by bit obliterating the existence of the old so that by the time the house was done, Kyle was nowhere to be seen. No hint of him in the bedroom, nor in the attic, nor in the living room, nor in the shed. He had been covered over like the hideous fifties wallpaper.

Sarah realised she was becoming more and more anal and obsessive. At her kitchen-warming party, she confessed to me that she'd called Kyle a useless prick because he'd put potato peel in the everyday bin. She hated how controlling she was becoming; she could sense that it was driving Kyle away, but she couldn't stop herself.

I gave her the number of a therapist my workmate Marj knew about. Sarah would come to my place after her sessions and debrief over a glass of wine. According to her, the therapist was in her early thirties, with kids — the photo was on her desk, and a loving husband — the photo was on her desk. For a huge fee she listened to Sarah talk. Apparently, they worked out together that Sarah had suffered a fractured attachment. This meant she had a really crap relationship with her parents. Sarah's mum and dad were divorced when she was a toddler. Vivienne Morgan was off filming for the entirety of Sarah's childhood and her dad stopped being her father after the divorce and started being her estranged father. Things hadn't improved when her stepfather arrived on the scene, and seemed to get even worse after he left, as her mother's fondness for a refreshment developed into a full-blown love affair.

Together, Sarah and the therapist worked out that Sarah lacked trust because of this fractured attachment. They worked out that Sarah wanted a baby most of all to right the wrongs of her own childhood, and that this was not healthy. They also worked out that

Sarah felt guilty, a little present from Catholicism.

Sarah told me she worked out all by herself that therapy was a very expensive way of learning to despise herself even more than she already did.

★　★　★

Talking to Kyle in his marital kitchen felt very uncomfortable. The Kyle I knew at university had pretty much disappeared and been replaced by Kyle the Mr Serious, Mr Works-Non-Stop, Mr Reads-His-Newspaper-Joylessly-And-For-Too-Long, Mr Why-The-Fuck-Can't-You-Get-My-Friend-Pregnant.

He'd had other parts to him in the old days, really nice parts, and that was why I'd been so excited when he and Sarah got together. As well as being incredibly fit, with the hardest calf muscles I'd ever felt in my life, he'd been smart, kind and hilariously funny, telling surreal anecdotes about couscous and pigs when stoned, and was unbelievably good at Pictionary.

After what seemed like an hour of small talk, Kyle left me in the kitchen and went to fetch Sarah. She emerged red-eyed and her lips started to quiver as she got closer to me. We hugged and talked and I apologised profusely and spoke soothingly.

When I got home, Sarah rang to say that she and Kyle had just had the most amazing sex and that it was a good thing for me to have said what I'd said.

I felt so sad for her, but I also wondered if moving permanently to their holiday cottage might not be such a bad idea.

3

You can understand that it was a big bummer for Sarah when I rang to tell her my news.

'I'm pregnant!' I said, still not quite believing it myself. 'I'm bloody pregnant!'

I shouldn't have blurted it out like that. It was part shock and part nervousness about her reaction. Also, I'd had a nightmare day taking a wee tot into care because her mother kept going to the pub and leaving her alone in the house. She caged Jess like a rabbit, with a bottle of milk Sellotaped to the rungs of the playpen for Jess to drink when she got thirsty.

At the Children's Hearing that day, I had outlined the facts of Jess's case and waited for the volunteer panel members to make a decision about whether to accept my recommendation to take her into care.

One panel member, an arse with a cowlick, probably no older than twenty-eight, with no children and no idea about parenting, was even more indignant with me than the mother was. While the mother sat and listened and admitted that she wasn't coping, he started attacking me, saying:

1. 'But the mother's admitting her problem.'
2. 'But the mother's willing to put in time with the social worker.'
3. 'How can we justify taking little Jess away from her mum?'
4. 'How hard will it be for her to get Jess back?'
5. 'Where will Jess go? Who will look after her? Do you have foster carers identified?' and
6. 'We must do everything we can to keep mothers and their children together.'

I was furious. The arse seemed to be more concerned about the mother than the child and this, more than anything, incensed me.

I'd always been drawn to children at risk. And despite not wanting to be a mother myself, I was opinionated about mother — child relationships. My own mum, I believed, provided a good role model of how to go about parenting. She'd always worked hard at providing friendship and boundaries for me, at keeping her own life while also devoting herself to me, so there was no unresolved bitterness on either side. Sarah's mum, on the other hand, had stuffed up Sarah's childhood good and proper. She was hardly ever there, drank too much when she was, had been divorced twice by the time Sarah was seven and was breathtakingly self-obsessed. The consequences for Sarah's self-esteem were dire. What do the Jesuits say? 'Give me a child until he is seven and I will give you the man.'

I believed I could spot flawed parenting a mile away, and felt it my duty to spare children from it. Social work was inevitable, I guess.

Anyway, I got my own way and two of the three panel members (the arse held out) agreed that the child should not be returned home.

Later, in the foyer, the arse with the cowlick said, 'It's difficult, isn't it, not being judgmental — but we should all try.'

'Yes,' I replied, looking at his face, and then down at his hand, which firmly gripped my arm. 'We should all try.'

He let go, and sighed as the mother handed some of Jess's things over to me for the foster carers. She wasn't even crying.

⋆ ⋆ ⋆

I'd headed straight to the doctor's from the hearing and it wasn't long before she decided my weight gain and exhaustion weren't the results of stress. A quick urine test put it

19

beyond all doubt. When I told Sarah I was in shock.

I couldn't believe I was pregnant. I'd had my periods every month, but my doctor explained they'd just been fraudulent, pretendy ones. Bloody lies! I was five months gone, and it was too late to do anything about it.

Sarah responded to my ham-fisted revelation by going silent and then hanging up. I spent a day arguing with her in my head about this. In cutting one-liners I told her how un-giving she'd been in my time of need and under no circumstances should I be expected to apologise or make the first move.

But I'm not so good at grudges, and after lunch the next day I phoned her from work and apologised.

She said she was sorry, too, and that she shouldn't have hung up, but my news had arrived at a terrible time.

It transpired that only an hour before I'd called, she and Kyle had been interviewed by a social worker to assess them for adoption.

'She's only twenty-one,' said Sarah, 'and definitely a lesbian. She sat on our sofa with her nose-ring in the air blethering on about my parents, for Christ's sake! I tried to show her around the house, but she refused. 'All in good time,' she said — and with a nose-ring!'

After I got off the phone I realised that the entire call had been about Sarah's ovaries, not mine, which to my ongoing horror were having a celebration dinner in my tubes.

*   *   *

Sarah and Kyle's adoption process grew along with my tummy. There were many more interviews with social workers, both with and without nose rings. Family trees were drawn, stories written, love — life/coping mechanisms/support networks scrutinised. Eventually someone ticked a box somewhere giving Sarah and Kyle permission to take on someone else's child.

We celebrated at Cafe Rosso with a bottle of chianti (yeah, I know, but at least my foetus wasn't on heroin like numerous mothers I had to deal with at work), three courses, and an argument about the Middle East. The perfect evening.

*   *   *

Sometime after our night out, Sarah collected a six-year-old foster child from their local social work office and took him home for the weekend. It wasn't the real thing, just weekend respite 'to break them in', Sarah said.

Kyle was waiting for Sarah and the child when they arrived, biscuits and diluted organic blackcurrant juice Sarah had bought at the ready, plus three DVDs about wildlife in Africa.

The wee boy took his place on the leather sofa with a cashmere throw, looked at the biscuits and juice laid out on the coffee table, and stared at Sarah and Kyle for several minutes. He had large green eyes and bright red hair and was as cute as a Glaswegian button. Sarah could have eaten him up, and Kyle started to feel quite manly having a boy who needed fathering in the house.

'Can I use the toilet?' the boy asked after a few minutes of awkward silence.

Sarah showed him to the en suite in his specially-painted-for-the-weekend room, shutting the door behind his delicate little features with the satisfied sigh of a loving mother.

He climbed out the window.

Before Sarah and Kyle had time to pour the organic juice into the specially-bought-for-the-weekend plastic-cup-with-groovy-straw, he was probably half a mile away. They had no idea until Kyle had watched all the trailers to the first African animal DVD.

After that Sarah decided fostering was a bad idea — irredeemable ginger underclass goods and all that. So she concentrated on the snail crawl of the adoption waiting list. And on me. She started coming with me to every antenatal appointment. She decorated my spare room, wrote endless lists of things to do, made mixed tapes for me to listen to during the birth, helped me write my drug-free birth plan, and cooked piles of freezable meals for afterwards.

* * *

At Sarah's urging I gave up work three weeks before D-day.

My colleagues gathered together to give me Marks & Spencer vouchers and a selection of cakes. My boss, who I soon learnt said 'fuckit' a lot, made a speech.

'Congratulations to Krissie and her husb — fuckit . . . I mean, by all accounts, you will make a great parent, mother . . . fuckit. Here's to Krissie.'

* * *

After leaving work, I decided that this motherhood thing might be bloody fantastic. I slept in, went for strolls, had lunch in cafes, watched *Quincy, ME*, read books, and ate at least one whole banana cake a day.

I laughed and laughed with my new

antenatal friends, dined with Sarah and Kyle at least twice a week, shopped with Mum and Marj, went to the movies. I bobbed along to aqua aerobics, ate curry, drank raspberry tea, gave in to desperate urges for cauliflower, and then, just as I was about to get bored, I gave birth.

4

It started when I was walking up the stairs of my Gardner Street close, eighty steps in total, breathing more loudly than I have ever breathed in my life. My face was raw, like a blind pimple that has been left to ripen the perfect amount of time and, if any pressure is applied, will pop a most satisfactory core. I had suffered the indignities of a vaginal probe when I bled at week twenty-two, of peeing my pants at week thirty-three when the check-out chick in Sainsbury's cracked a very funny joke, of farting in front of my 'Ms Has-No-Body-Functions' colleague when I bent over at work to pick up a case file, and of fainting during a 'cervical sweep'.

At nine months and ten days pregnant I fully expected an explosion of water. What I didn't expect was to bump into twenty-nine-year-old bass-playing Marco from downstairs.

I'd been flirting with Marco for about a year. One night I was listening to him and his mate jam through my floorboards and I decided to knock on his door. 'You need a bit of rhythm,' I said, before waltzing in to join them with my tambourine.

An awkward hour or two followed as I realised that the evening was purely about music, and not about drinking, smoking, flirting or talking. I said goodbye at ten and, though they seemed really pleased I'd joined them, the whole situation had made me feel a little unsure of myself, so I went home to self-hate with a bucket of ice-cream, like the Americans do.

I often bumped into Marco after that, and we'd chat on the stairs for a few minutes. He'd ask me how my rhythm was going, and I'd say fine, and I'd ask him how the songs were coming along and he'd say fine, and all the while I wondered why he didn't seem to notice the smouldering sexual tension between us.

As time went on and my tummy got bigger, we'd play a game of who can ignore the increasing belly before us. We'd look each other straight in the eye and talk seriously — 'How is the rhythm?' 'How are the songs coming on?' My gaze would be so determined that any attempt by him to move his eyes in a downwards direction would have been positively illegal.

On this occasion, however, the sexual tension and anxious eye gazing were inter-rupted by an audible pop.

'What was that?' asked Marco.

'I think it's my mucus plug,' I said.

I left Marco dry-retching on the stairs, went into my flat, took my pants off, examined them, and phoned Sarah.

★ ★ ★

Sarah arrived about half an hour later, having already established with the midwife that I should not come in till things 'got serious'. I discovered later that this meant I should not come in until I felt so out of control with pain that I could kill myself and/or others.

For four hours Sarah played me tapes, made me tea, massaged my back, and ran me baths.

'These are a piece of piss!' I said as I breathed correctly through an irregular tummy twinge. 'I could do this forever!'

I'd always had an inkling that I had a very high pain threshold. I didn't like blood, but I could handle pretty much anything else. As a kid, I hadn't cried during any of my immunisations. When I broke my nose windsurfing, I was calm and steady and sensible even though it was the worst fracture the doctor at Stirling hospital had ever seen. I never understood all the fuss about period pain. Other women appeared to me to be wimps. And I regularly found bruises on my legs and had no idea where they'd come from. All sure signs that I had a superhuman tolerance to pain.

But the irregular tummy twinges turned to regular stomach pains and the regular stomach pains turned to agonising never-ending cramps, and the agonising never-ending cramps turned to earth-shatteringly incomprehensible poundings, which made me want to kill myself and/or others.

It was time to go to hospital.

I can see why they say you forget the pain of childbirth, and that it's not so bad, and that at the end of it, all that matters is the bundle of joy you're holding.

They say it because they are lying bastards.

I will never forget having a huge set of knitting needles inserted into me by a student nurse who wasn't sure if she could feel my cervix at all, let alone break it to set my waters free. I will never forget several fists 'examining' me in the fourteen hours that followed. I will never forget a huge set of steel salad servers somehow barging their way inside me and yanking so hard that my bed flew across the room. And I will never forget being rushed to the theatre after all that, after Sarah had made sure my birth plan was followed to the letter, because my placenta was quite happy to stay put, thank you very much.

What I have forgotten is what Robbie looked like when he came out. I don't remember. And when I came back from surgery, I didn't ask where he was. And when I slept that night, I didn't hear him cry. And when I woke up the next morning and someone placed him on my tummy, and his mouth found its way onto my nipple, I didn't forget the pain of labour and I didn't feel that I was holding a bundle of joy.

I felt like an alien was sucking on my tit.

5

Sarah stared at Krissie with a mixture of awe and fear. She couldn't believe Krissie had actually done it. Krissie had a child, who was now crying in the cot beside her. Krissie herself was lying on her back, watching the ceiling, the bottom half of her hospital nightgown covered in blood. Sarah was surprised that the nurses hadn't helped her to maintain her dignity, although she, of all people, knew how busy nurses were.

Krissie's face was ghostly white and spookily vacant. She didn't seem to notice the baby's crying nor Sarah hovering over her, perplexed.

'Krissie! Congratulations. You clever clogs. Kriss!' said Sarah, kissing her on the forehead. She put flowers, magazines and fruit juice on the bedside table, and sat down.

'He looks like Mike Tyson,' Krissie said after a while, her voice uncharacteristically flat.

Sarah had to admit that he did look a bit battered. The forceps had obviously pulled him by the temples, and both were squished in and bruised. They'd also scraped his eye as they tried to get hold, and his left eyelid had a small gash across it.

When Sarah picked Robbie up and, still crying, he looked at her with tiny little dark piercing eyes, she felt them go straight through her and a shudder of emotion filled her to the brim. She cried. And as soon as she cried, Robbie stopped crying. Just stopped and looked at her, as if to say, 'It's okay, it's okay. I'm here now.'

They say you really fall in love for the first time when you have a baby, that you're breathless and crippled with love. That would have been how Sarah felt — an overwhelming peace and warmth, a tingling ache of fulfilment — if she hadn't had to hand Robbie to Krissie to be breastfed.

Sarah watched the two of them for a moment. But her lip began its signature quiver, and she couldn't take it. It was so unfair. She had to go.

When she got home, Kyle was reading the paper.

'How'd it go?' he asked. 'Boy or girl?'

'Who gives a shit?' Sarah said, and went to bed.

★   ★   ★

Kyle couldn't recall exactly when it became normal to be spoken to like this. There was a

31

time when it would have seemed odd for his partner to call him 'useless', for her to hide in her room and surface only to groom or feed.

If ten years ago someone had said to him, 'Kyle, in ten years you will live in a very tidy house with a wife who seems to despise you and who comments frequently and some-times in front of people that you have left sticky skid marks on the side of the toilet *again*,' he would have found it hard to believe. After all, he was Kyle McGibbon, who got on with just about everyone. He was a doctor. A catch. He had hair and, genetically speaking, a good chance of keeping it. He was slim, and almost always managed an erection.

'No way!' Kyle would have said to this unlikely prediction. 'If anyone treated me like that I'd trade her in so fast she'd still smell new!'

But he didn't trade Sarah in, mostly because of the great years they'd had before trying to conceive. Years of going to the movies; of waking still linked in bed and smiling. Kyle wondered if the smiling would have continued if his poor wife hadn't turned mad with the need to reproduce. He'd watched her disappear in front of him, like a dying patient, and all he could do was provide the palliative care of income and shelter.

Year one of the bid to have children, Sarah's voice changed from soft and loving to snappy and not. Kyle tried to respond with patience. 'Sarah, please don't speak to me like that, darling,' he'd suggest politely, after his premenstrual wife had pointed a stiff threatening finger at him and said, 'I hate fish cooked in tomatoes! You know that, you idiot!'

Year two he attempted relapse prevention strategies, organising a mystery mini-break for the weekend before Sarah's birthday. It was Prague and it went very well, but the actual birthday a few days after their return was terrifying.

'Nothing's wrong, Kyle,' Sarah had said, 'except it's my birthday and I'm watching the *X Factor* with a glass of stale Morrison's merlot and YOU MEAN TO SAY LAST WEEKEND WAS *IT*? NOT AN ENTREE BUT *IT*? WHAT DID I DO TO END UP WITH THIS LIFE? I'D RATHER BE THAT FAT BIRD WITH LEARNING DIFFICULTIES STANDING IN FRONT OF SIMON COWELL THAN MARRIED TO SOMEONE WHO DOESN'T EVEN LOVE ME ENOUGH TO GET ME A DECENT PRESENT!'

Year three Kyle tried to fight because his mate Derek had started to call round regularly, and as it turned out he was also married to a psychotic bitch. 'Don't put up with it!' Derek said. 'They're all bampots with their own agendas and you have to nip their control freak antics in the fucking bud!' So one night Kyle told Sarah not to put his papers out for recycling till he'd finished reading them. Then he poured himself a beer and put football on in the formal living room and when she switched it off he got up and turned it back on, and when she turned it off and looked at him with those eyes he decided that it would still be fighting back to go and drink his beer and listen to the match on the radio in the shed.

Year four he just stayed in the shed as much as he could.

'I'm turning that fucking pit-hole into a gym!' Sarah yelled. 'How are we ever going to conceive if you shut yourself out there in the dark like a mole? Honestly, Kyle, you've gone all peely wally from the lack of light and you've got a beer belly. It's disgusting! You're going to have to take me from behind.'

By year five — the seventh year of their marriage — the life had been sucked out of him, and he spent as long as he could at work or at the gym. The rest of the time he walked a tightrope, hoping only to make it to the end, to not fall off.

6

At first I thought it was the baby blues. I'd heard that on day three (when your tits transform into granite boulders capable of hitting innocent passers-by with shots of warm milk), you can get a little teary. This is the perfectly normal baby blues. So when I cried because the breakfast lady had no apricot jam, I didn't panic. This was the baby blues. Perfectly normal.

But on day four I cried because no matter how hard I tried I could not find my pelvic floor muscles. On day five I cried because I was beginning to face up to the fact that one day I would have to do a poo. On day six I cried when I did the poo and on day seven I cried at a Cornflakes ad on the telly. On day eight I cried when I went home with my slightly-less-yellow child. He'd had jaundice, which had made him very yellow and meant we couldn't go home till day eight.

In the third week I cried every time my mum came over because I felt like I was the stupidest and worst mother in the history of the world.

'Maybe you're depressed? It's quite common,'

she whispered nervously on one occasion.

I was holding Robbie against my rigid, tense nipple and grinding my teeth at the time. 'You go have a nap,' she ventured, watching Robbie wail as he tried to extract juice from my brick. 'Then afterwards, maybe we could ring the health visitor, or Kyle, together?'

'I'm fine,' I snapped.

She didn't give up, bless her. She left pamphlets about postnatal depression on side tables. (I threw them out.)

She got Kyle and Sarah to visit me. (I talked about the weather.)

She just happened to show up at the same time as the health visitor. (I talked about the weather, which was fine, like me.)

I was always 'fine, fine, fucking fine!' God, if I wasn't fine, then what kind of woman was I? The kind that's a failure. The kind that doesn't deserve to be a mother.

When all else failed, she and Dad took Robbie and I to Italy for some rest and relaxation. I have never found anything so stressful in my life — filling in Robbie's passport application form without touching box-edges; holding him up in a photo booth so he was the right size, shape, colour; finding decent law-abiding citizens to verify his identity on the back of the photos; standing in an emergency passport queue somewhere in town while he howled; packing clothes for two not one — nappies and wipes and things I'd never had to pack before; standing in airport queues with my parents, who could not disguise their worried faces.

We stayed in a five-star hotel with a pool and an award-winning restaurant that overlooked the breath-taking Lake Como.

It was awful and I was awful. I argued with the hotel manager about the air-conditioning, with the bus driver for not helping me up with the pram, and with Mum and Dad about everything else. It was the opposite of rest and relaxation.

After we got back from Italy, I took Mum's advice and decided to invite my antenatal friends over. We were all around the same age, we'd all had jobs and lives, and being together had been a real giggle during our pregnancies.

But when they arrived it felt to me as if something weird had happened to them since they'd given birth. They were not only *not* a giggle, they seemed to have changed into competitive witches.

'I'd never let him sleep in the bed with me!' said one of the mums.

'The trick is don't let them get away with it,' said another.

'At six weeks most of them sleep through, although my Zara is already sleeping all night.'

'You're very highly strung, aren't you, Krissie?'

Worse still, they moaned on and on about their men, smugly oblivious to the fact I'd have given anything to have another adult in the house to talk to, to share the burden with, to love.

But their men were apparently all useless lumps of lard who:

Followed them around the house trying to get it, but they were not going to get it, oh no.

Did not seem to understand that evening pints down the road were a thing of the past.

Needed management, because they have no idea, honestly . . .

Poor bastards. If I'd had a man to share nappies and arguments with, I was sure I'd be the antistereotype: grateful, loving, easy-ozy, and willing to give it, oh yes.

They left just in time, because if they had stayed any longer I would have screamed even louder than their perfect, cretinous babies.

★   ★   ★

Mum was probably right about the postnatal depression, but I couldn't or wouldn't see it. I couldn't see anything for the black cloud that had suddenly fogged my world.

Six weeks came and went and there was no sign of Robbie sleeping through. I'd go to bed and pray that he would, but he never did, and so neither did I. Instead I entered the dark hole of sleep-deprivation-psychosis where everything is dreich and miserable and pointless, even chocolate.

My morning routine had changed from Lavazza and bath, both frothed, bright GMTV tidbits before leisurely stroll through architecturally exciting streets with trees, to dealing with crying peeing shitting leaking eating messing dressing messing and redressing.

Zara's mum — we no longer had names, we antenatal women, we were 'Zara's mum' or 'Beth's mum' or 'Robbie's mum' — Zara's mum phoned at this point and said not to worry if Robbie wasn't sleeping well, because three months would definitely be a real turning point. Most of them 'give back' at three months and everything falls into place she assured me.

At six months Robbie still did not give back, and I realised I didn't even know what 'giving back' meant. I rang Zara's mum to tell her this and she said, 'Well at nine months things will be a lot better.'

'I don't believe you!' I said. 'You've lied to me twice already!'

When she suggested I really should talk to someone, I said, 'That's what I'm doing, I'm talking to *you*, but what's the use in talking to you if you're just going to lie to me?'

She hung up.

★   ★   ★

After another month of this I decided to go back to work and absolve myself of daytime responsibility. My increasingly anxious parents supported this decision and were happy to help out with Robbie, who they'd well and truly fallen in love with.

Each morning when I arrived Mum and Dad would open the door and give me a hug, clearly worried about me, but not wanting to say anything to upset me. They had food and milk and proper care and attention at the ready, and I would hand Robbie over and cry all the way from Kenilworth Avenue to the Kingston Bridge.

★   ★   ★

It didn't help, going back to work. First day back, I was dying to talk to Marj. As well as being a great pal to have lunch with, Marj had been my weekender, the chick I went out with on Saturdays, the one who thought I was the funniest girl she'd ever met, who'd always guffawed at my fabulous mock reasons for chucking boys, including:

Peter Fischmann had an outie.

Rob Bothwell spat his prune pips onto my plate.

Giuseppe Conti did not have a car.

Jimmy McGeogh gave an inappropriate standing ovation.

Jonathon Miller was married.

I sat down at lunch that first day and Marj made the mistake of asking how Robbie was. 'Well, last night he slept from eight till ten, then woke to feed, and then slept from twelve to four-thirty, which wasn't bad, but I couldn't get back to sleep after that and ended up waiting for him to wake up at seven for his morning bottle, so I'm a bit tired.'

I had never seen eyes actually glaze over before — but I could have put a cherry on top of Marj's. And it began to dawn on me that I was as boring and moany as my antenatal friends.

After the first week, Marj realised that my world had narrowed alarmingly and I had no other stories to tell. I started eating lunch at my desk the following week and discovered Marj's new Saturday pal was a girl called Tilly

41

who'd just split up with her man, Toby, because he'd sent her a professional portrait photograph of himself.

Each morning, I felt like I'd worked a full shift by nine-thirty, and I would spend the day in a cyclical wasteland of forgetfulness. I would sit at my desk staring at my over-filled diary and then, as if someone had yelled, 'On your marks, get set, GO!', I would bound from said desk with all the purpose of a champion hurdler and stride out of the room, only to stop, bewildered, halfway along the corridor. Why had I left my desk? I would then walk backwards and try to retrace my steps. Usually, I'd just forgotten that I needed a pee.

I began to wonder how I'd ever managed the job. Before long, I had thirty cases: five children on the child protection register, another ten in care, and the rest on the brink of being taken into it. I had angry parents yelling at me on the phone, or waiting to yell at me in reception. I had admin staff refusing to type reports for me. I had managers with questions I couldn't answer — 'What did the head teacher say about the carpet-fitting knife, Krissie?' 'Were the leg burns fresh?' 'Calves swollen?' 'Did she actually buy some pork sausages?' 'Was it blue or yellow valium?'

I got home late most nights, having visited houses to talk in riddles.

'Do you mind if we come in?' (We're coming in.)

'An anonymous source said Rachel was on the step for an hour last night.' (You are guilty of child neglect, and your neighbour is watching.)

'I can see needles under the television.' (You're a liar.)

'Do you mind if we take her with us for the night?' (We're taking her, no matter what you say.)

When I finally got home after work, I would spend the night worrying about Jimmy Barr's uncle who was getting out of prison, about Bob being beaten, Rob being touched, Jane being left in her buggy outside the pub. It was the hardest, most relentless of jobs, and I had lost the strength to cope with it and the confidence to judge others when my own parenting was so crap.

After a few weeks of stopping, puzzled, in corridors and lecturing bad parents about safe drug use and appropriate boundaries, I fainted.

Sarah picked me up from work that day, then rang my mum and asked her if she and Dad could look after Robbie for the night. After some hushed conversation between the two of them, Sarah put me in the spare bed in her beautiful house with a happy film and a hot chocolate and a kiss on the forehead.

As I lay there watching television with soft warm lighting and no baby, I loved Sarah more than I had ever loved her. Sarah, who always looked after me, always protected me.

And when she told me the next morning that work had agreed that I should have a break and that she and my parents had agreed it would be good if they looked after Robbie so that I could go on a camping holiday with her and Kyle the following week, I loved her even more.

7

Something changed in Krissie when she woke the next morning. Perhaps it was having a full night's sleep, perhaps it was the idea of a week in the Highlands with no responsibilities. Whatever it was, she felt different, she felt good, and she was going to make some changes, be a better person. She formulated a good-mother strategy in her head that involved sacrifice, greater patience and eventual joy.

After breakfast with Sarah, she decided to go shopping. An autumn wardrobe would help her pick up Robbie with a fresh face. Afterwards, she would take him to the park and they would feed crusts to the ducks and play with crunchy red autumn leaves and laugh.

Shopping was not a success. Krissie had a new body and did not know what to do with it. She collected size tens from the racks in H&M fully expecting that most of them would look good, only to find that three of the trousers did not make it past her thighs. She wondered why the hell her thighs had changed shape — the foetus had been nowhere near them.

Krissie returned to her parent's house in Kenilworth Avenue at three that afternoon, determined to implement her good-mother strategy. She packed Robbie into her car and drove to the park. When she got there, Robbie had fallen asleep, but she took him out of his seat and put him in his buggy because that was the plan. She walked a still-sleeping Robbie to the duck pond and threw two bits of bread in the water, which sank. After taking a photo of Robbie sleeping in the buggy with her mobile phone she walked through a soggy scattering of yellow leaves. Then she walked back to the car, put Robbie back in, which woke him up, and drove home to her flat.

Robbie cried all the way.

As soon as Krissie got inside, she poured herself a red wine. A clean nappy for Robbie came next.

Krissie had a sip of her wine and put Robbie into his high chair. She then sat down at the table beside him, drank the rest of the glass, looked at him and put her head on the table in exasperation at herself, her inability to cope, her abject parenting skills.

Then she felt something on her out-stretched hands. She lifted her head and saw that Robbie had grabbed her fingers and was holding onto them tightly. He was looking her in the eye and laughing. The two things were connected — the hand-holding and the laughter. He was talking to her, telling her that he liked her, and asking her to hold his hand.

But she didn't hold his hand. She poured herself another glass of wine.

After the fourth glass, she put the empty bottle under the sink and realised with horror that there were at least a dozen empty bottles there. She told herself that these had taken a long time to accumulate and that it only looked bad because she was saving a bootful for the bottle bins near Asda.

Then Krissie put Robbie to bed. It wasn't like in the movies, Krissie thought to herself, when parents kiss a forehead, turn off a light, stand dotingly at the door and then walk away. Putting Robbie to bed was more like storming the shores at Gallipoli: scary and futile.

She had tried the antenatal mums' consensus of strict routine: food, stimulation — but not too much, bath, bed. It didn't work. She'd tried depriving him of sleep during the day. Nup. Tried sleeping with him. (It worked but she made the mistake of telling Fraser's mum who said: 'NO! He will die if you keep doing that. Didn't you hear about the baby who suffocated!') So Krissie turned to her latest hardback childcare purchase, *Controlled Crying*, which told her to reassure him, leave him to cry, then return at increasing intervals throughout the evening. 'After one week, your baby will sleep through!' the book had promised.

This was day six, and Krissie very much suspected that she might need to ask for her money back. She had left Robbie for two minutes, returned to reassure, then four, returned, then eight, returned, sixteen, returned, and here she was, retreating from the darkened room for the fifth time like a burglar, praying that Robbie would not notice that his mother was decreasing in size and then disappearing out the door for thirty minutes this time.

'Go somewhere far away,' the book had advised. 'And be strong!'

Until now, Krissie hadn't been able to, but today was the first day of her new life as a resolute, capable, loving, boundary-setting mother, so she was determined.

Outside the bedroom, Krissie heard music coming from downstairs. She hadn't heard the boys play for months and the sound sent a rush of excitement through her. Without giving herself time to think, she put on some lip-gloss, grabbed the baby monitor, set the alarm on her watch for thirty minutes, and went downstairs.

When Marco answered the door she said, 'I haven't got my tambourine, can I rattle something of yours?'

Marco replied exactly as she'd hoped. He seized her around the waist and kissed her. He then looked at her monitor, from which Robbie's voice was wailing.

'Don't worry, he's fine,' she said.

They staggered into the hall, and into the bedroom, and then Marco lifted up her skirt.

The pain surprised her. It was sharp and piercing, and as he penetrated her a snapshot of midwives and blood and large metal salad servers flashed before her. What had happened down there? Had they sewn her up a little tighter than before?

The sound of Robbie's crying whirled out of the monitor and around the room and she looked at her watch over Marco's bobbing shoulder . . . He'd only been crying for ten minutes. She shook her head and returned her attention to Marco, who gave three quick shoves before he was done.

Afterwards they walked into the living room, where the other lad was playing his harmonica. He didn't acknowledge Krissie at all.

'You sure he's all right?' Marco asked,

grimacing at the screaming monitor as he handed her a shaker.

'Yep, don't worry,' Krissie replied, turning the monitor down a bit after looking at her watch.

Without another word or glance in her direction, Marco picked up his guitar and started playing.

Krissie felt humiliated. What had she done? What was wrong with her? She didn't know what to do, what to say, how to behave, so she sat there and shook her shaker while the baby monitor howled an agonising harmony. The seconds pounded on her watch, but she would not give up, she would wait the full thirty minutes. She would be a good mother.

★　★　★

Sarah arrived at Krissie's house at nine o'clock. Concerned about how her friend was coping, she'd decided to drop in.

She knocked once but there was no answer, only the sound of Robbie crying. She phoned Krissie's mobile, which she could hear ringing inside. She rang the landline again, but it rang and rang. Sarah banged on the door. No response. Mindful of Krissie's fragile state, Sarah phoned the police.

The siren made the boys stop playing, and

when the siren stopped the alarm on Krissie's watch started going off. It was time to reassure. She jumped to her feet and ran upstairs.

When she got to her door, Sarah was standing there.

'What are you doing here?' Krissie asked.

'Where were you? I called the police! Quick, open the door,' Sarah said.

'What? Why? He's fine!' Krissie said as she turned the key. She went into Robbie's bedroom and saw that he was bright red with panic.

'Hey!' Krissie said, picking him up. 'Hey, it's okay, it's okay.'

Tears came to her eyes, seeing him like that. What had she done to him? She rocked him gently, and for a fleeting moment she understood him, that he was lovely, that he liked being held in her arms, that only his mum could calm him down. She cried with him, her lips against his tiny ear. 'I'm here, I'm here.'

'Controlled crying,' she explained to Sarah. 'I was trying to be strong, like the book says. I had the monitor.'

An incongruously pretty young police-woman knocked on the door a few minutes later. 'Everything okay?' she asked when Krissie answered the door.

'We're fine. I was just downstairs briefly. Doing controlled crying, you know, teaching him to sleep. I had the monitor on and was heading back up when Sarah arrived and called you.'

'Controlled crying? That's a nonsense if you ask me. You're better off putting them in bed with you,' the too-pretty cop said, before heading out the door.

'Shite, I'm so stupid! I'm so sorry. Shite! Shite! Shite!' said Krissie, tossing her childcare book into the bin and carrying Robbie into her room.

8

When Sarah left me that night I brought
Robbie into the bed with me. I felt guilty. I
would try harder, I told myself. Okay, so the
first day of my attempt to be a good mother
had been a disaster, but I shouldn't give up. I
decided as I lay there that I would hang out
with him more, play with toys on the living
room floor with him, make Santa beards in
bubble baths, don clever voices at story time.
I would do all of these things, selflessly and
with great pleasure.

I gazed at him breathing gently beside me
on the bed — so wee, so perfect, so helpless
— but then I worried I'd smother him, like
Fraser's mum said, so I lay rigid, my right
arm tingling with pain, listening to the hours
click over on my alarm clock.

★   ★   ★

I still had a week to go before the holiday. On
the first morning, I woke to a wonderful
five-second oblivion, where everything was
numb and painless. Then with a stretch I
remembered what I'd done the night before.

I'd left Robbie alone to shag an idiot neighbour. And that was me trying! That was me being a good mother! I sighed as I looked at him gurgling beside me on the bed, completely dependent, completely at my mercy.

It took me two hours to get us fed and dressed. I then bumped the buggy down four flights of stairs, one slow step at a time. My back was aching when I reached the bottom. I opened the heavy front door but it swung shut before we'd managed to get out. I spent several minutes trying to extricate us, to the amusement of several unhelpful passers-by, and then walked in the rain along three main roads filled with pot-holes and students who seemed physically unable to see babies. Drenched and exhausted, I dragged the pram backwards up the steps into Kyle's surgery.

Kyle looked different there. Official and serious. I'd never seen him at work and his stiff-backed awkwardness would have made me laugh had I not been there to talk about my terrible failings.

'Postnatal depression is not a failing,' Kyle said. 'It's very common. And it's good you've recognised it.'

He printed out a piece of paper and I have to admit that the whole thing did make me feel better, knowing I wasn't alone, that there was help, that I deserved and needed a break. Even the paper itself with its lovely little druggie words made me feel better.

The day after that, Robbie and I made play dough. It would be lying to say I enjoyed it, especially cleaning up afterwards, but I started to understand that there was something dreamlike about slowly kneading flour, salt, oil and colouring, and something funny about having your nine-month-old baby squash your yellow elephant.

The next day I lay on the living room floor beside the baby gym, looking up at the squeaky bright things Robbie was chuckling at, his wet mouth wide open, before I drifted off to sleep.

The day after, I pushed Robbie's swing and then jumped on the one next to him, and I may have even felt a tinge of joy when our eyes met.

But there was no understanding and no joy the next day, because I had to pack Robbie's things, and this daunting task had expanded in my head to the point that it was oozing out my ears. I was sweating and shaking by the time I was ready to take him over to Mum and Dad's.

'Have you brought his formula?' asked Mum.

'Has he had a morning nap?' she asked.

'Has he tried solids yet?'

Has he got a good Mummy?

I kissed them all goodbye. As they shut the front door a mixture of guilt and relief overwhelmed me. By the time I got to my car, the guilt was gone. I was going to have some adult conversation. I was going to get some fresh air. I was going camping!

★　★　★

Camping! I loved it. Loved the baked beans, the smell of the campfire, the scary stories and the huddled stinky sleep. As I drove home I remembered the last time I went camping with Kyle. I'd come home from lectures one evening, sick to death of sitting in semicircles or breaking off into small groups, and exclaimed to Kyle and Chas: 'Let's go camping!'

I grabbed my two-man dome tent, my gas cooker, foam mattress, sleeping bag and light. Kyle had driven us in his rich-boy Mini, our gear spilling out of the boot. Chas sang all the way along Great Western Road — funny, silly little songs that he knew every single word to. We laughed so hard at him, Kyle and I, but not so much when we realised that his repertoire could carry him all the way to Loch Tay and back. He sang around seventy

56

different songs, I reckon, without even a tiny break. Tunes about Mrs McVittie having only one titty and wishing Campbelltown Loch was whisky, Cambelltown Loch och aye.

He was still singing when we erected the tent in the rain, still singing when we realised the gas cooker was out of gas, and still singing after we ran a mile, only to find that the food at the local pub was 'aff'. So we had vodka for dinner, and crisps, and I fell on the tent after a midnight barf and it collapsed on Chas and Kyle.

It was the funniest, best night of my life, and I found myself laughing out loud as I packed the tent the next day, even though it still smelt of cheese-and-onion puke.

9

The night before they went camping, Kyle had spent two hours sitting on the bed watching Sarah try on her hiking gear. The boots matched the Tiso trousers perfectly, he had to admit, and the jacket-with-cute-pocket was surprisingly well cut, and the raincoat did fold perfectly into the side pocket of the Goretex rucksack, and Sarah had indeed done all the tasks on her list of things to do.

He thought wistfully back to camping trips with Chas and Krissie. They'd once decided to go camping for the weekend at five o'clock on a Friday night and were on the road by five-thirty. He'd packed a cagoule and matches, Chas had packed a quarter ounce of Dutch skunk. Krissie had hardly packed anything besides chocolate. It couldn't have been more different to this.

Kyle was almost sweating with relief by the end of Sarah's fashion show. He'd said all the right things, and was now allowed to go and read his paper (which had been placed in the recycling bin). He wasn't always so lucky. Once, when he'd had a hard day and wasn't thinking straight, he'd told Sarah the truth about a pair of shorts. 'Maybe they shrank in the wash,' he said, before shrinking into a tiny ball of regret himself.

Kyle was used to feeling regretful by this stage.

He regretted that Sarah was failing in her desperate attempt to build a different life from the one her mother had slapped together for her. She had it all mapped out — the stable home, the holiday house, the babies, the hard-working parents who would stay together and always be around. As time went on, Kyle realised he was witnessing a losing battle, because Sarah didn't have the wherewithal to build a different life, didn't have the role models or the confidence. She was trying to do brain surgery with a spoon.

When Sarah had arrived at Kyle's flat years before he'd been immediately besotted. She was the most beautiful woman he'd ever met and he spent most of the next nine months looking at her. He'd gaze at her while she was sleeping, look into her eyes across restaurant tables, and smile at her in shops while proudly noting the shopkeepers' awe.

But the infatuation had long died away.

Back in their student days, when Chas was proclaiming the truth about beauty, he said: 'Some folk get uglier the more you look at them, whereas some folk get more beautiful.' This was true, Kyle now knew, because Sarah's perfectly symmetrical face had become less intriguing over the years. She had slightly too much flesh at the sides of her mouth, which time and an extra stone had accentuated. At thirty-three, she looked puffy. It wasn't only that, though — there was nothing striking in her eyes, nothing sparkling in her smile, nothing that he wanted to spend time looking at.

Krissie, on the other hand, had many things he wanted to look at. Sitting on the sofa beside Kyle, with Krissie doing sit-ups on the living room floor, Chas had said, 'When I first met Krissie, for example, I thought she was a dog.'

Krissie hit him, pinned him down on the ground and began tickling him.

Through screeches of wonderful ticklish pain, Chas continued, 'But now, I think you're the most beautiful woman in Glasgow.'

'Where?'

'Scotland.'

'Where?'

'Okay, okay, the universe! Stop!'

Krissie then looked at Kyle and raised her

eyebrows questioningly.

'I still think you're a dog,' said Kyle, jokingly.

Kyle hadn't really thought Krissie was a dog. And now he thought she was the opposite of a dog. Over the last ten years, her boy-body had, when in 'functional mode' become a lean, perfect female specimen, and when in 'going out mode', it could have been used on the Paris catwalks. Her features had metamorphosed into captivating elegance. She seemed to throw outfits together within seconds and come out looking both sexy and comfortable.

Chas had also said that women always, without exception, become their mothers. And this had proved true. Sarah had become Vivienne Morgan, the-stage-actress-turned-soap-star, last seen in the Glasgow soap *The Lake* for a three-episode story-line involving a long-lost mother, but best known for her work in the eighties power-drama *A Life for Rizzo*. In her prime, Vivienne Morgan was sex on a stick. Now the 'stick' was more like a large vodka-filled trunk, and the 'sex' was two round balls of silicone perched beneath an implanted, injected face.

Sarah had inherited personality traits from her mother such as a 'fix-it' approach to life. For instance, Sarah's mum did not talk to her daughter about periods and sex. Instead, after she noticed the stain on the back of her daughter's school uniform, she sent her off to the chemist, alone.

Krissie's mum, on the other hand, was a sixty-three-year-old hill-walker with rosy cheeks, a beaming smile, a nicely thought out wardrobe and a 'let's talk about it' approach to life.

Why had Kyle been so blind? Why had he fallen for a woman who was destined to be as miserable as her mother?

Other things Kyle regretted included buying the house on Loch Katrine, which Sarah expected him to work on non-stop. He regretted following in his father's footsteps and doing medicine, because he did not like hard work and being a doctor was hard work. There was no way of skiving, even as a GP, and he was constantly plagued with guilt and self-loathing because he had no ambitions to study or write or further his career. He wanted the opposite. He wanted to leave and take people on skiing trips. But he could never do this. Doctors can never leave.

And when Sarah decided not to talk to Kyle for two whole weeks, refusing to pass him both the salt and a message about a vulnerable patient needing to be seen immediately, he regretted telling her that her shorts were too tight.

After Kyle left to dig his paper out of the recycling bin, Sarah packed her perfect camping clothes in her perfect rucksack and smiled. Things were in order.

Therapy had helped her to admit that she was a control freak and that her aggressive perfectionism was a reaction against the adults whose behaviour towards her had been less than perfect — her mother, her father, and her stepfather, Mike Tetherton. What therapy hadn't clarified was: what was wrong with being a control freak? What was wrong with having things in order? If things were in order, and if it all went according to plan, Sarah might succeed where her mother had failed. She might keep her man and build a happy family.

10

Mike Tetherton had tried escaping once before. He'd left his wife, Vivienne, and his stepdaughter, Sarah, and had boarded a train.

Now, as he sipped on his hot chocolate, and placed the thermos safely on the grass, he felt the same way he had when the 2.40 to London had pulled away from Glasgow Central twenty-seven years earlier. He was excited, but nervous as he looked at the South Ayrshire countryside around him — the rolling green hills which meandered towards the coastline. Moving his deckchair to face the sun, he sat down on the chair, which was poised smack-bang in the middle of a fenced plot of land in the middle of nowhere. This was Mike's dream — to be totally and wonderfully alone, away from the gossipy commuter town where he had lived for years, away from the cutthroat world of filmmaking. Away from temptation.

Mike Tetherton looked younger than his fifty-nine years — he could probably pass for forty-five — and his features were smooth and cheerful, the mouth turned up slightly, the eyes smiling.

After taking another sip of his milky drink, he closed his eyes, and breathed in deeply. As his lids opened, he soaked in the empty, warm Scottish countryside. This was to be his new life, his fresh start.

But first he had a decision to make. He had paid the deposit on the plot months earlier, and wanted to build a minimalist German kit house made mostly of glass. But he could not decide where to place it. Which direction should the living room face? What would he see from the French doors in his bedroom? Should the sun set over the decking or over the forest? Would the trickling of the stream in the valley be more soothing in the bedroom or in the eat-in kitchen?

Following the advice of a home show host, he'd brought a chair with him the first Sunday after buying the land. He'd sat on the chair for a few minutes so he could begin to imagine where the house should go. After the initial embarrassment of sitting still and alone, Mike had settled into it and found the experience illuminating. He drove home that night knowing exactly where his house should be positioned — diagonally, one-third of the remaining land at the front, two-thirds at the back, the kitchen facing south-west.

But when he came back the following week, he sat down for a cup of hot chocolate in a different position. He was straight on, directly in the middle of the land, the kitchen facing due south. As he watched the sun move into the evening he felt confused. This position also had its merits.

The weekend after, Mike tried a few other spots, and sat at each for a bit longer.

After three months, he was still sitting on his chair for several hours at a time, staring at views that might possibly be the views of his future.

★　★　★

Mike was 'in-between jobs', and he busied himself during the week with community projects. Everywhere he went people gravitated towards him. His smile, his dog and his willingness to help, seemed irresistible. It was tiring, being so nice, and as Mike folded his chair yet again and placed it and the thermos in his twenty-year-old Mercedes, he sighed, no closer to a decision about his escape, and headed back towards his hectic, helpful life in Drymlee.

And sure enough, there were three messages on the answer phone and one neighbour at the door before he could even unpack. 'Mike! Good news,' said his elderly neighbour Netty. 'The Pirates have won!'

This *was* good news. It meant the community had beaten the developers, and that the green patch across the way, Greensleaves, would not be littered with luxury two-bed apartments but with swings and slides for the local children. Mike and Netty had campaigned hard for this, planning the site, getting quotes, organising workmen, standing at the council's buildings with placards held by several kids. Mike had been interviewed by the local radio station and spoken impressively about the need to provide communities with facilities to glue them together. For decades the acre of green had provided kids and dogs with space to express themselves, said Mike, and this should not be taken away.

So the Pirates had won, which meant Mike had a hard week of physical labour ahead of him, having been elected project manager of the pirate-themed adventure playground.

Three cups of tea later, Netty closed the door and left Mike to do what he needed. Unpack. He was anal about this. He'd learnt over the years how to close a house for several days, taking exactly what was needed for a trip away, and how to prepare a house for homecoming so that 'Aah' is the reaction, and not 'Jesus, shit, when will I ever finish that ironing?!'

Mike put a load of washing on, placed his suitcase in the eaves cupboard, and looked out the window at the greenery opposite. He loved this flat. It was private and bright and, while his view was fresh and panoramic, no-one could see into his windows at all. Next Mike ordered his shopping online and ran a long bubbly bath. He then surfed a while longer before attending to the three messages on his answer phone.

The first was from his ex-colleague Paul, a cameraman who'd worked with him on several documentaries. Paul had heard a rumour that the BBC was looking for ideas for a new series aimed at teens. They should get together, he said, at that Italian place in the West End, maybe.

The second was from the builder who was interested in the job if the Pirates won, and could start immediately.

And the third was from a neighbouring housewife who took her job as treasurer of the residents' association as seriously as she took baby massage and cello tuition.

'Congratulations!' she said. 'We are all so very grateful! And the pup's been fine with us; come get him when you're ready.'

Mike's puppy was a black labrador that, to Mike's consternation, shat and peed all over the place.

Mike would get him later. Right now, he needed a bath.

⋆   ⋆   ⋆

Over the next week it was mayhem at Greensleaves. Mike had arranged for the acre to be levelled and the diggers had scraped the land flat, leaving a huge pile of earth at one end that had turned to mud with the rain, and which six or seven kids were tobogganing down with windswept faces.

He'd felt a little weird lately. Maybe it was tiredness from working on the playground. Organising workmen and harassing suppliers had been hard and for a week he didn't finish till ten at night. He'd not even had a chance to walk his dog. Netty and her granddaughter, Isla, had taken over this duty, and he was glad of it. But he was becoming a little paranoid. Since working on the site, he often felt the treasurer of the residents' association, Netty and several other neighbours were looking at him oddly, that they had been talking about him. He hated feeling this way. It was pathetic. But he did.

'Get over here, Isla!' Netty yelled from the window of her flat across the road to her granddaughter, whose uniform was dishevelled and covered in mud. 'Your mother will be furious!'

Isla waved back at her gran with a grin and Netty couldn't help but smile back at her.

'Lucky she's away for the weekend!' Isla yelled.

Mike gave six-year-old Isla a high five as she ran back towards the muddy hill where the other children climbed and descended with gusto.

'Okay!' Mike yelled to the group at the top of the mud pile. 'First one down wins a pound!'

Mike smiled as the screams of excitement and pleasure trailed behind the children.

⋆   ⋆   ⋆

The following morning was Saturday and Greensleaves had been temporarily abandoned for family time involving Ikea and arguments. Mike had no role in this so he packed his car to head south. As he packed, he could hear his dog barking inside Netty's house, scratching at the door to be let out. Mike had dropped the puppy off a few hours earlier, because Isla was staying for the weekend and had begged to look after him.

'That dog,' thought Mike.

He made a flask of hot chocolate, packed sandwiches, cake, fruit, his chair and sunscreen, and put his house in order — online shopping done for his arrival back on Sunday, plants watered.

As he drove out of Drymlee, he knew today was the day that he would make the decision. All he had to do was get the builders out and point somewhere, and they would pour the concrete foundations, which would solidify. End of story.

He had just set up his deckchair on the plot when his mobile rang.

'Hello?'

'We got the gig!' It was Paul, the cameraman. 'We're in pre-production as of Monday.'

'My God! Fantastic!'

Mike hung up and took a deep breath. He then walked towards his car and drove fast along the country road, taking several roundabouts, and rejoining the road north. Excitement brimmed inside him. This business, it was addictive. Like an alcoholic on his way to the off-licence with money in his pocket, Mike was about to be relieved of a tingling and everything else would just have to wait.

Mike left his deckchair on the land, sitting in the field in the middle of nowhere, empty.

* * *

71

Netty was on the landing chatting to her downstairs neighbour, Jim, when Mike returned. Jim owned a comic-themed shop in Glasgow and told everyone an enormous amount about it. 'I have a vision that one day there will be Daffy mugs in my shops all over the central belt!' he'd said to Mike the previous week. But they were not talking about Daffy when Mike approached his front door. He was sure of it. They were talking about him, and they hardly even tried to hide it.

'Mike!' Netty said. 'Jim's just saying what a fabulous job you're doing over there. We honestly don't know what we'd do without you!'

Mike chatted as openly as he could. He had nothing to hide, despite their apparent suspicion. The traffic was terrible through Glasgow. He'd just heard he'd landed a documentary. The playground would be finished in a week tops. The weather had cleared up, yes, and as Isla poked her head out of Netty's front door he reassured her that his premature return did not jeopardise her pup-sitting for the weekend. She squealed with delight as Mike's little labrador bit at her legs energetically and then ran to his owner for a scratch.

'Let me put that begonia in my side

window. It needs to face south for a bit,' Mike said, shooing the pup back to Isla with his leg, and waving farewell to his neighbours.

'Thanks,' Netty said, handing over the plant to Mike. 'Oh, and Mike,' she said, with what seemed to him knowing eyes, 'it will be finished for Guy Fawkes, yes?'

'Absolutely.'

'So we could all meet down there after tea? For fireworks?'

'Of course.'

Netty sighed as Mike went inside. After her divorce at fifty-six, she had reached the conclusion that all men were bastards and she had lived happily with this truth for sixteen years. But then Mike moved in — good-looking, polite, helpful, honest, emotional Mike — and this had thrown her theory to the wind.

Mike shut the door and also sighed. Here we go again, he thought.

11

Here I go again on my own,
Goin' down the only road I've ever known,
Like a drifter I was born to walk alone . . .

My iPod was on full blast and Glasgow was whirring by my window. I'd arranged to meet Sarah and Kyle at Milngavie Station, a thirty-minute train ride from home. I had missed travelling alone. No-one on that train knew who I was; no-one knew I had a recently stitched vagina and a nine-month-old baby. I was just a girl on a train with an iPod. Things were looking up. I was going to be all right. The sun was shining and even the suburbs of Glasgow with their grey pebble-dashed bungalows looked nice.

The music started giving me a headache after a few minutes and I had this sudden fear that Sarah and Kyle wouldn't show up. I sensed Sarah's disapproval of the controlled crying fiasco. She probably thought I was a bad, ungrateful mother. She'd refused to leave that night until I'd had a shower, a coffee and two hours to sober up. I'd cried a lot and apologised, so I thought we'd left on good terms, but maybe she hated me.

Surely they would show up. They had to.

Much to my relief, Sarah and Kyle were waiting for me on the platform. They ran towards me, smiling, and we all jumped up and down on the spot a couple of times like schoolchildren, linked arms and danced in a circle, and then got some guy with long matted hair and a grey-blue rucksack to take a photo of us in front of the sign that marked the beginning of the West Highland Way. I hadn't seen Kyle giggle for years. What a difference! This was going to be the most incredible holiday, I thought to myself.

Which was true in the end.

We walked to the leafy suburb that edged the city and bounced alongside squirrels in a large country park. For several hours we meandered with the lush flat farmland, and then sat by a burn and ate fresh banana cake and drank hot chocolate prepared by Sarah that morning in a whizz-bang thermos. A whisky distillery was beside us, Highland cows were in the fields adjacent, and we felt like we were on the set of a Scottish tourism ad.

Over lunch we traded stories about people Kyle and I had gone to uni with.

'Chas was so in love with you,' Kyle said.

'Rubbish,' I replied.

'You knew! He followed you around like a puppy dog!'

'You're full of shite, McGibbon.'

After Chas dropped out of medicine and started working and taking drugs, we still lived together and had lots of fun, but working and university seemed like different universes back then. A while later he disappeared to God knows where without even saying goodbye. When he materialised afterwards he was a bit weird with me and almost immediately ended up in Sandhill Prison.

It was Kyle who broke the news to me.

'You'll never guess who got eight years at the Old Bailey!' he said over the phone one evening.

I don't normally do things that are a waste of time, like reading joke emails or guessing, but Kyle hounded me. 'Guess, go on, you never will . . . '

'Um, Ewan McGregor.'

'No.'

'Your mum.'

'Nup.'

'Your dad.'

'My dad's dead.'

'Oh, shit, sorry . . . (Pause) . . . He is not dead!' I remembered.

'It's Chas, you dick. Chas!' said Kyle.

I was gobsmacked. Chas was so gentle he befriended ants, and had never so much as stolen a sweetie from the corner shop as far as I knew.

'Why? What'd he do?'

Kyle didn't know much. It was attempted murder, he'd heard, something to do with an incident at a tube station involving a shopping trolley. Chas had gone mad, what with all the drug-taking, obviously. Rumour had it he'd brandished the trolley proclaiming to know the truth about this and that.

Kyle and I suspected that he may well have known the truth about this and that because Chas was always right about everything. What we couldn't grasp was how he got a shopping trolley through the turnstile at Angel underground, down two sets of escalators, and what he actually did with the trolley once he was there. Did he ram the passengers? Add them to his basket?

After they transferred Chas from London to Glasgow, I visited him three times. This wasn't easy, as I couldn't just show up. Chas had to arrange his own visits, then ring and let his visitors know when to come. But he didn't ring me or write. I sent him several awkward letters, not wanting to be overly jovial so as to remind him of what he'd lost

and send him off the third-floor landing in B
Hall, but not wanting to be underly jovial
either, so as to remind him of the
meaninglessness of life and send him off the
third-floor landing in B Hall.

Hey Chas,

*I'm sitting in the university cafe and it's
pissing with rain and even my chips with
curry sauce seem dull. I miss you! I don't
understand why you won't write back, but
please do, and please arrange a visit. I want
to ask you about what happened, tell you
what I've been up to.*

*Please ring me. I'm in most evenings
(life is very boring for me at the moment). I
can visit any time as I now spend all my
working day in the car, stopping occasionally to steal children, and could easily slip
away for an hour or so.*

*Enclosed is £10 for your phone card.
Please call!*

Take care, Chas,
Krissie

After several weeks of similar letters, I turned
to Plan B, which was a devious and cunning
plan involving overcoming prison security by
infiltrating the agents' visits area. In other,
more prosaic, words, I would tell the prison

officers that his social worker was here to see him.

I was sweating like a pig by the time my ID, bag and thumbprint were inspected and I was allowed inside. The guards intimidated me, sure, but not as much as the mutants in the waiting area. It became clear as I glanced around me that Sandhill housed a specific demographic and that the prison was simply an extension of their patch. They seemed to share expectations. Their sons would inevitably end up here at some point, and the guards would talk to them like pieces of shit. Poor dental hygiene and a unique turn of phrase designed to terrify newcomers were also shared.

Eventually, the locals were ushered into the visits area and I was ushered into agents'.

'Charles Worthington, Prison No. 15986, B Hall, 3/36.' I wrote this on my request sheet, having cleverly bypassed prison security and accessed its database (I rang Records and they told me), and then took my place in room seven, a glass box with a table and two chairs.

I waited an eternity underneath the corner cameras in the interview room, worried that they would catch me out. I was not a criminal justice social worker. I was child protection, and I had no place here. I was an intruder and I would surely be caught and hanged in the old hanging cell in D Hall and then buried in an unmarked grave with the others out the back.

Each time a red or green polo-shirted body was uncuffed in the area I wondered if it might be Chas. I hoped to God he didn't show up with a green polo shirt because I knew these were the shirts worn by the beasts in D Hall.

He wore red, and while he looked skinny and drawn, he still managed to pull off the outfit with some flair. Larger red polo shirt than the other guys, maybe, that flowed well from his muscular chest then down. And even though his denims were unfashionably even-coloured, they did not appear as tapered as the others. When he saw who it was he tried to turn around and leave, but the uniformed brute at the end of the corridor pushed him back towards me. He reluctantly came over and sat down, his eyes moving downwards and staying there.

I shuffled my papers and began the mock interview.

'Hello, Chas, my name is Krissie Donald. I'm a criminal justice social worker and I've been asked to complete the Home Background Report. The aim of the report is for the Parole Board to get as much information about you before deciding about early release. First things first, let me check I have the right details. You got eight years. If you've been a good boy, you'll be out in four. Your offence is . . . ?'

Chas did not answer.

'The crime you committed is . . . ?' I looked up at the cameras and smiled nervously (did they know I was lying yet?).

He said nothing.

'Okay, now if you do not cooperate with the report you do realise that this will not look good when it comes to a decision . . . '

No response for several seconds. My heart was beating so fast and my palms were so sweaty I knew it was just a matter of time before they burst in the door and yelled, 'Right, up against the wall, you and you. Don't say a fucking word, you gobshite pricks!'

But no-one came in. Instead, Chas leant across the table and said, 'They can't hear you, they can only see, and only if they're looking, which they're usually not.'

'Jesus, why didn't you tell me?' I breathed in for the first time in minutes.

We smiled at each other, but then both our smiles melted into something not so smiley.

'How are you, Chas?'

'Great.'

A pause.

'What are you doing here?'

'Well, each morning I have PE and three afternoons a week I study anger management and in the evenings I watch Sky movies with my cell mate Rab, who sometimes meows and sometimes doesn't.'

With this, he stood up and walked out of the room. I realised I couldn't yell after him like I would in the normal world. If I did, alarms would ring and the keys of a hundred nearby officers would jingle and Chas would find himself at the bottom of a large pile of blue polyester uniforms. So instead I gathered my papers, my dignity and my powers of deception, and left the way I came.

I tried the same thing again, twice, but he refused to see me.

I rang his parents. They lived in Morningside in Edinburgh and were extremely nice. 'All we know is he got into a fight, hon. It breaks our hearts that he won't see us, our lovely boy. You've seen him? He looked okay? Oh, thank God, it's agony. Our little Chas.'

Mum — who'd always had a thing for Chas — said maybe he had his reasons, that he was a good friend and a good person and maybe he just needed some time. And time he got.

★ ★ ★

As Sarah, Kyle and I packed our lunch away we talked about Kyle's other pals from uni, who were now zillionaire plastic surgeons or award-winning world savers. I felt like I was chatting to Kyle for the first time in years — wee soul, he obviously felt as plagued with self-loathing and disappointment as the rest of us. He always looked a bit out of place alongside his medical friends, I thought. They were doctors from birth. They had plans. They wanted to save patients and live in mansions and give withering looks to frivolous people. I always thought Kyle should have been one of the frivolous, like me. He worked hard, but when he took time off, he played even harder, as though he was making up for lost time. During the summer he'd smoke dope with Chas, watch crap television, and read Lonely Planet guides over and over, as if backpacking by osmosis. I believed that medicine dragged him down and gave him a frown that he never should have had.

Aware that Sarah might be feeling left out, I started chatting to her about old friends, when the lad with the matted hair who took our photograph on the train platform walked by. We asked him to join us but he said he couldn't, as he was going to head up a hill. He was doing an extra climb every second day because the ninety-six-mile walk from Glasgow was not painful enough, apparently. Funnily, the man with the matted hair was called Matt.

He said he'd love to see us that night, though, and he wrote his mobile number on a piece of paper and gave it to Sarah before smiling at me and walking into the distance with an inordinately good bum.

Sarah said it was déjà vu.

We were good Catholic schoolgirls, Sarah and I. Our parents had gone to great lengths to ensure our tickets to heaven, sending us to a nun-run private school. When we graduated to secondary, we got the train home together and talked about boys. Before long we had graduated to talking *to* boys.

We used to change trains at Glasgow Central, so Sarah and I would wait for our connection in Burger King. The boys from St Aloysius would sit at Burger King too, and relationships developed which went like this:

Boy would give Boy's Best Friend a note, and Boy's Best Friend would give it to my Best Friend (Sarah), and the note would read: 'Will you count bricks with me?' My Best Friend would read the note to me and I would smile in full view and coyly write 'yes' and she would return the note to the Boy's

Best Friend who would pass it on to the Boy.

I would then make my way to the low-level train platform and stand with my back against the wall and wait for the Boy to waltz towards me, put his hands against the wall, do an open-mouth-no-tongues kiss, and this was us counting bricks.

Sarah never counted bricks. She was too pretty and had no intention of wasting time on wee neds in Burger King. So instead of counting bricks, Sarah would listen to them placing bets about whether or not I'd let their mate get a Cap'n Birdseye.

Even then she remained pretty protective of me. In fact, when she went to nursing school, and I went off with my rucksack, I really noticed the difference. There was no-one to stop me, so I went hell for leather, and now should anyone ask, I'd have to round my tally down to the nearest ten.

All these years later and Sarah was still looking out for me the way she had at Central Station. The only difference was that at sixteen I didn't let anyone get past second base, but at thirty-three a home run was pretty much guaranteed.

My sexual awakening had occurred between the ages of fifteen and nineteen in seedy low-level train platforms (as above), in rusty sheds, in back lanes and in scout hall bathrooms. In each venue I would be a quivering mess, as I stopped the hand from going *there*, slapped the hand as it tried to go there, let the hand go a little bit nearer to there . . . Oh God!

I would pray in church afterwards, saying thirty-three or so Hail Marys, and later worrying that I should have rounded it off to an even number or added the odd Our Father. And this wasn't even full-blown sex! These prayers were for 'tweaking' and 'fingering' — the first term referring to the rubbing of nipples to the point of rash, the second to the relentless prodding of teenage digits in all the wrong places. God knows, if I'd done the whole caboodle, I'd have been praying all day.

I don't know when my Catholicism left me, but it did. Soon after, I stopped lying to Mum and Dad about going to mass, and eventually — just to make sure they knew I was really lapsed — I got pregnant to some fellow in a Tenerife toilet.

What I realise now is that Catholic guilt gave me the best sex of my life. I had at least five years of refusing to go the whole way with my devoted boyfriend. What I would do now to have someone like him work on me day in, day out, work and work and work! I will never find such attention, motivation and dedication again. And I will never feel such scintillating sinful guilt. When I think of that boy — his name was Stewart — I think of someone with incredible knuckles.

After I told my folks that not only did I not know what Father O'Flaherty said in his sermon last Sunday, but that Father O'Flaherty was probably sleeping with his housekeeper, and that I had no intention of going to mass ever again, I went through something of a moral revolution. I put guilt about sex in a box, wrapped it up, and threw it away. Instead of going to mass, I decided to do nice things on a Sunday, like bike-riding and shopping — and I banged away at pretty much anything, ever-skilled at not getting too close. I decided that I should not worry about being respected. Sex was sex was good and proper and I figured any guy who thought a girl should be respectable was a chauvinistic waste of space anyway.

★   ★   ★

As we walked from our idyllic lunch retreat towards Loch Lomond, I wondered if my moral revolution had been ill advised, if I'd gotten it all wrong. I was a single mother. I hadn't had a long-term relationship since I'd split up with Stewart at nineteen, never having properly consummated our relationship. I was lonely as all hell. Would things have been different if I'd stayed respectable?

12

Sarah had known for a long time that she and Kyle needed to get away, though her idea of 'getting away' was more along the lines of an all-inclusive bubble-wrapped five-star resort with hundreds of people in similar clothes. Her favourite holiday memory was of Dubai, where she and Kyle had been allocated their own private section of the swimming pool to lounge in all day. She had plenty of time of an evening to buff and fake-tan, and the risk of nail breakage was negligible.

Sarah's therapist had suggested that she let Kyle take control a little more, but when Kyle told her he'd organised a walking trip in Scotland she'd wanted to throttle him. She was not the sporty type, and had spent most of her childhood making up excuses to get out of PE. She'd never camped in her life and worried for many nights before they left about the logistics of her ablutions. Usually, she packed two suitcases for a break of any length, but Kyle had confiscated her hair-straightening tongs, electric toothbrush, Clarins cleanser, toner, night moisturiser and day moisturiser. He'd whittled her luggage down to one rucksack.

But walking in the sunshine through the quaint villages south of Loch Lomond, she decided that maybe this was exactly the right holiday for them. As Kyle and Krissie laughed about their old friends, she decided it probably was. After everything they had all been through, the fresh air and exercise and beauty of the trek was just what they needed. On that first day, Sarah was surprised to discover she felt happy, and went for seven hours without making a silent prayer.

Sarah hadn't lost her faith like Krissie had. Every Sunday she went to mass and prayed for things to happen or change or be better. She'd then say sorry for anything she might have done that made things not happen or not change or not be better. She truly believed that Mary was a virgin, and that God and Jesus had an elusive relative called the Holy Ghost. And she believed if she prayed hard enough everything would work out. She would be fulfilled.

Each Sunday after mass, Sarah would go home to Kyle feeling positive and enlightened. She was part of something big and great and this big and great thing would look after her. She'd cuddle up to Kyle on the sofa and touch his collar seductively and try not to think about making a baby. Then she'd accidentally initiate sex, and spend the following week not thinking about her period, and the week after that not thinking about her period, and when she was officially overdue fifteen days after the sexual encounter, she would not think about her period so much that she felt ill with a sickly combination of powerlessness and hope. Of course, her period came. It always did.

It's when an overwhelming disappointment like this happens that Catholicism really kicks in. It lets you be angry and unreasonable because as long as you pray, as long as you seek forgiveness, any kind of behaviour is okay. So Sarah would spend at least a week being angry and unreasonable — her prayers became expletive-filled thrashings; her seduction techniques were more like self-flagellations, using Kyle as her whipping rod. In such circumstances, Kyle started to find it difficult to produce the seed his wife craved.

Sarah knew Kyle was a good man, the first good man she'd known properly, and she'd stopped worrying about his lack of ambition. She'd stopped being angry at him for their childlessness. It wasn't his fault, apparently.

But at some point, her love for Kyle had started to wane. It hadn't happened all of a sudden. Her love faded a little bit more with each piece of bad news — whether it was delivered by a period, a failed fostering attempt, or an unchanged position on the adoption waiting list. Their love for each other was evaporating. They both knew it. And they also both knew that one more piece of bad news would leave them both dry.

⋆ ⋆ ⋆

A red sun was setting over Loch Lomond when they arrived at the campsite, which was nestled between the loch and the hills and was full to the brim with muddy, badly-dressed, heavy-drinking walkers.

Krissie, exhausted but proud of having walked so far, dropped her rucksack on the shore with a satisfied sigh. She noticed Matt setting up his red tent a hundred metres away, and nodded so slightly she wondered if he noticed, so did it again less slightly, then wished she hadn't as it was obvious he'd noticed both (desperate) nods.

Sarah had a shower in the camp bathrooms. Her feet were red and her legs were aching and her new rucksack had cut into her shoulders, so a long hot shower felt fantastic. After that she dried her hair with the compact hair dryer she'd smuggled into her rucksack when Kyle wasn't looking.

Meanwhile, Kyle and Krissie got the tents

up, no hitches at all, and collected wood together to start a fire. By the time Sarah came back from the bathroom, they were sipping wine in its glow.

'You did not bring your hairdryer!' laughed Krissie.

'It's not easy, looking as good as I do,' said Sarah, smiling as Kyle handed her a mug of wine.

Sipping his wine, Kyle wondered how it was easy for Krissie to look so bloody good, having spent no time on ablutions at all. She was covered in sweat and dirt from the wood and her hair was stuck to her head and her knee was scratched from a fall on the bank, but she looked gorgeous.

As Kyle moved on to his third mug of wine, he stared at Krissie. What with the relationship with Sarah having gone so awry, he had not had sex for months, had not so much as masturbated, and his balls were heavy with the burden of it. He had never talked to anyone about this because he found it mortifying.

As he sat looking at Krissie over the fire, he remembered having sex with Sarah and this calmed him a bit, because in the latter stages it had been truly dreadful. On one occasion when Sarah had been taking fertility tablets of some sort, he'd just given an elderly patient a prescription when his pager went off. 'There you go Mrs Beattie, take that to Boots,' he said, escorting her to reception.

'Tickityboots?' asked Mrs Beattie.

'Take it to Boots. Boots!'

'What about them?' Mrs Beattie asked.

Kyle handed the befuddled Mrs Beattie over to his receptionist and read the message from Sarah: 'Here, now!'

When Kyle arrived ten minutes later, Sarah was lying on the bed with her T-shirt on, trousers off, and underpants shoved to the side. She couldn't even be bothered to take them off. She swiped some KY onto herself and then said hi. Most guys might have had trouble maintaining energy in this scenario, but Kyle nuzzled in for the duration, imagining himself to be with anyone else.

That was one of the last times they'd tried to conceive, and sex had seemed kind of sad since then.

Kyle stopped looking at Krissie and turned to Sarah. As she sipped her wine, years of tension and worry seemed to have been replaced by bright cheeks and enthusiasm. Kyle caught a brief glimpse of the woman he fell in love with, the woman who didn't call him an idiot, who didn't leave lists of jobs for him to complete by a certain date. She was smiling, and her whole face changed with it,

94

came to life. Kyle felt a slight flutter, seeing her fresh and out of context, and wondered for a moment if he could return to a previous time, when her smile was the only thing he needed.

13

I rang Matt while Sarah, Kyle and I were playing 'face up'. We were pissed after three bottles of wine, and we dared each other to face up to our worst fears.

I'm a big fearty when it comes to bloody injuries so Kyle dared me to cut his hand so that it bled enough to paint one small tissue red. He told me not to worry, he was a doctor, and he'd stop me if I went too far. Handing me his Swiss army knife, he then held out his hand. My sweat glands got to work immediately, as they always have, as I took his hand in mine. Warm sweat poured from my palm onto his. He pushed the blade of the knife tightly against his flesh. It was never going to work and I started to feel dizzy. I hesitated and looked Kyle in the eye. While I was doing this, he moved his left thumb under my hand affectionately and a sudden surge of adrenalin made me shut my eyes and cut into him.

'Jesus!' yelled Kyle, recoiling with pain.

I watched the blood spurt from his hand . . .

'Krissie! Krissie! Kriss! Hello! Are you okay?'
Sarah's face was blurry as it came into view.
'You fainted.'

She helped me sit up and it took a few
moments before I fully regained consciousness and remembered what had happened.
Kyle held up his hand, which was fine, and
dangled a bloodstained tissue in front of me
with a huge smile.

'It is SO your turn!' I said to Kyle.

Kyle had always been an arachnophobe. He
cut his gap year in Australia short after an
incident with a hairy huntsman, and jumped
when a spider so much as showed itself on
television. I always thought this girly attribute
was rather fetching. I liked it when men were
vulnerable, when the macho facade melted,
which is probably why I liked it on top, and
why I secretly had a fantasy about watching
two men doing it together.

Anyway, I set about finding the largest
spider in the vicinity. It took a while, but
eventually I spotted one about five centime-
tres across, sitting happily between two
branches of a rowan tree. He turned to flee
from me, but I managed to scoop him up.
Kyle closed his eyes and held out his hand,
but as soon as he felt a tickle on his palm, he

catapulted backwards and squealed like a baby. I wonder if the spider made it back to the rowan tree, or if he became some kind of spider refugee.

Sarah was next. Her greatest fear was being confined in small spaces, so we put her in her sleeping bag, did up the zip, and told her to stay there for ten minutes.

'Don't forget!' she said, as the zip closed in around her.

That was when I rang Matt. He'd climbed his hill, and was just about asleep in his tent. 'Get up and get over here,' I said.

As I hung up, I saw the photo I'd taken of Robbie in his buggy, sleeping soundly by the duck pond, and I rang Mum.

Robbie was fine, they were all fine, Mum told me. I shouldn't worry about a thing.

Kyle poured me another wine, and we chatted for a while before realising that fifteen minutes had gone by and we had left Sarah in her sleeping bag.

'Shit! Sarah!' I said, and turned towards the sleeping bag. It was motionless.

'Sarah!' I said loudly.

No movement or response at all. I slowly unzipped the bag, and opened it out. There, white as a ghost, eyes closed, and still as death itself, was Sarah.

'Sarah?'

Nothing.

I shook her.

'Sarah!'

Not a breath, not one sign of life.

'Kyle! She's not . . . moving.'

Kyle dropped his drink and moved closer. Our faces moved towards her until we were about one centimetre from her. What had we done? Had we killed her?

Way worse than my fear of blood was my fear of doing something really bad, of hurting someone unintentionally. I would have my terrible actions on my conscience forever. I would have to go to jail, or worse, not go to jail because I'd not confessed or not been caught, and so I would have to just live with the guilt all by myself in a dark smoky room with eerily vacant eyes and bedraggled hair . . .

'AAGGHH!'

Sarah's scream sent us both flying into the air. When we picked ourselves up from the ground, she laughed so hard that we could only stop her by tossing her into the loch. When she surfaced with an angry face we knew we'd overstepped the mark. Nervousness overcame Kyle and he held out his hand to help her out. Sarah took it, and then hauled him in with all her might.

What the hell, I thought, and jumped in

too for a splashy, giggly, freezing swim.

We were still splashing about when Matt arrived. It was an unseasonably mild night, but not mild enough to wear next to nothing, which is what Matt wore. He'd taken off his yellow T-shirt that said I AM NOT GAY! in black italic lettering and walked along the jetty beside us, stood over me with a smile, and then dived in.

I'd promised myself earlier that day that I must try to be respectable and that I must never again sleep with a man on the first date, but as Matt swam over and pushed my head under the water playfully, I decided that holidays and Matts must surely be an exception.

We dried our clothes by the fire and drank beer. Sarah and Kyle snuggled up in the firelight and seemed so relaxed and in love that I hardly recognised them.

It was nice to see them like this, but after five minutes or so I gave Sarah long significant stares, which she didn't seem to notice. I started getting a bit annoyed that they were hanging around for so long chattering away, and then, when Sarah asked how Robbie was, I nearly died. Why did she want to stuff it up for me when Matt and I were obviously well suited?

To my shame, I clarified the Robbie

comment to Matt with: 'He's my budgie. Mum had to take him to the vet.'

After the long uncomfortable silence that followed I had to say something.

'I'm off to bed.' I turned to Matt. 'You coming?'

He seemed surprised, and then delighted as I took his hand and walked him towards my tent.

14

Kyle watched as Krissie pulled Matt towards the tent. When Matt bent down to go in, she put her foot on his bum and kicked him inside, then jumped on top of him before she'd even zipped the tent flap three-quarters shut.

Kyle looked at Sarah and raised his eyebrows. Krissie's sexual aggressiveness was nothing new. She'd always been 'proactive', as she called it, and she put up a good feminist argument as to why this was okay. But having known and liked Krissie for so long he'd always wondered about the pathology of her particular combination of promiscuity and lack of emotional commitment to the men she slept with. It wasn't as if she came from a dysfunctional family. Quite the opposite, in fact — since both her parents were delightful and very loving.

Even more striking were her close friendships with men like him and Chas with whom she didn't have a sexual relationship. She'd always been oblivious to how much Chas loved her, determinedly keeping her relationship with him playful but platonic. It seemed to Kyle that Krissie never entered into sexual relationships with men she actually liked.

After raising her eyebrows back at him, Sarah unleashed some long overdue bitching. 'I can't believe her,' she said.

'What do you mean?' asked Kyle.

'Last week she shags a neighbour, leaving her baby alone in the house. Tonight she pretends Robbie doesn't exist so she can screw the brains out of some other dope.'

'She's depressed,' said Kyle, as Krissie's naughty giggles ricocheted from the tent.

'How can you defend her?' asked Sarah, before going to their tent in a huff.

Kyle did feel protective of Krissie. She was finding it hard to be a mum — what single mother wouldn't find it hard? She was all alone, and had not completely anticipated the responsibilities of motherhood. Plus, she was a free spirit, a creative spirit with dreams and passion and excitement. Of course it was hard.

He was getting pretty hard himself, Kyle noticed as he tried to stand up to go to the tent. He looked at his semi-erect penis and quickly sat back down. He'd been thinking about Krissie, and this was what had happened to him. Was he developing feelings for her? And why was he looking at the unzipped part of Krissie's tent, where he could see a tiny piece of flesh, and feeling so discomfited? And why didn't he stop looking? Why, instead of stopping, did he crawl along the ground, closer to the gap, commando-style, his semi now becoming fully detached, and park himself one foot from the zip so that he could see more bits of flesh moving in the darkness?

Kyle was not a premature ejaculator. He had always been quite proud of his 'yardage', which was a mathematical equation he and Chas had developed that went like this:

Y = t 3 l

or:

Yardage = total number of thrusts 3 length of erect penis.

Anyway, Kyle's was good. Good length, good number of thrusts per session = good yardage. (Chas calculated that his was even better, but Kyle guessed this was probably to do with anti-depressants which stopped him from coming, although he had no proof of this.)

But by Loch Lomond that night something happened to Kyle that hadn't happened since he was thirteen when he and Annette McMillan exchanged a look. He ejaculated, after the slightest rub against the raw earth beneath him.

Kyle let out a surprisingly loud gasp as this

happened, and promptly heard Krissie stop what she was doing to say, 'What was that?'

Kyle ran into his tent, jumped into his sleeping bag and snuggled up against the sleeping Sarah a split second before Krissie could be heard outside asking, 'Did you hear something?'

'No,' said Kyle drowsily, as Sarah stirred beside him.

'I thought someone was outside my tent.'

'Not us.'

'Okay then. Sorry about that. Nighty night! Thanks for a fantastic day!'

'What's she on about?' Sarah asked sleepily.

'No idea.'

A pause.

'I'm sorry,' said Sarah.

'Me too.'

'I love you.'

'Me too.'

Sarah kissed Kyle, but he rolled away.

15

I was determined, after the painful experience with Marco, to enjoy Matt, but it happened again. As we connected, the pain was excruciating and images of blood and crying and retained placentas rushed in at me. About then, I heard a gasp, as if someone was outside the tent. I halted proceedings, put my top on and went outside, but there was no-one there. I asked Kyle and Sarah, but they didn't know anything about it. It seemed I must really be crazy. Not only was I a depressed alcoholic who had flashbacks, but I was also paranoid.

I returned to Matt and told him I was drunk and spinning, and that I didn't want to have sex with him anymore. I also told him that I didn't have a budgie. I had a baby boy, Robbie.

'Och, don't worry,' he said. 'Come here you, let it all out . . . Let it all out.'

So I did. I cried into his chest.

And then he let it all out. Undid his zip, took my hand and slapped his sticky flesh into it.

'Jesus!' I pulled my hand away and tried to

get up, but he pulled me back down and lay on top of me, kissing my neck and forehead with a furry, dry tongue.

'No!' I said a little more loudly, but he kept going.

'Matt! Stop!' I shrieked.

I tried to push his chest, but he didn't seem to feel it. All he seemed to feel was between my legs, and I didn't want him there. I wanted him gone.

Before panic really set in, Matt fell on top of me, and as I shoved him off me Kyle came into view, bending over us.

Kyle dragged Matt all the way to the loch and pushed his face into the water. I followed, surprised by Kyle's anger and strength, and watched as he held Matt's head down. I was too dazed to do anything at first, but after a few seconds I realised I needed to intervene or Matt was going to drown.

'Stop!' I said, but he didn't.

'STOP!' I grabbed Kyle's shoulders and shook him and he finally made eye contact with me.

'Let him go,' I said.

As soon as Kyle dropped him in the water, Matt scrambled to his feet and ran off into the distance. He must have packed up there and then, because his tent was gone in the morning and we didn't see him on the track at all the next day.

Afterwards I sat beside Kyle on the loch. We didn't say anything at all, just sat there and stared, and then Kyle stood up quietly and went back to his tent. I don't know how, but Sarah slept through the whole thing.

After Kyle left, I stayed by the loch and thought hard. I'd asked for it, hadn't I? I'd been rat-arsed and I'd literally dragged the man into my tent. What was he supposed to think?

I watched the huge body of water in the loch move with the wind. It looked scary and unfathomable. I was feeling the same way about my life: it was dark and cold, and I was lost in it.

★　★　★

The next day Sarah woke up fresh-faced and well rested, while Kyle and I staggered out of our tents tired, hungover and grumpy. We all had baked beans and coffee for breakfast and packed our tents. Kyle and Sarah didn't make a good tent-packing team. When it came to the folding, Sarah kept going left instead of right, and then right instead of left and, well, she was just plain useless. After several attempts at folding the tent small enough to fit into its teeny tiny tent packet, an exhausted-looking Kyle asked Sarah (huffily) to make some rolls for lunch, which I was already doing, and she (huffily) came and sat beside me.

★ ★ ★

It was a little overcast as we began the walk along Loch Lomond. It was going to be another long day's walk — over twenty miles — so we had to keep up the pace. We started reasonably well — me first, Kyle next and Sarah behind. But after two hours or so, Sarah stopped to rearrange her pack, and by twelve o'clock she had not only finished all our water, but had taken to stopping every twenty minutes.

We sat on a beach and had a lunch of rolls and ham and, my God, I would have killed for a drink of water, but like I said, Sarah had finished it all, so I dipped my head into the midge-filled loch and sipped a worryingly still mouthful.

I suppose what I felt at lunch that day was anxiety. My heart had started pumping a little fast, and my whole body felt like it had just woken up after a night of heavy drinking with only three hours' sleep — which wasn't exactly surprising, since it had. My head felt fuzzy, eyes sore, adrenalin pumping, blood sugar levels all over the place. As I looked at Sarah eating the roll I'd made her, I wanted to scream at her: 'I hate the way your jaw clicks when you eat!' As I was thinking this I caught Kyle's eye and could have sworn that he was thinking exactly the same thing.

'Penny for your thoughts,' said Sarah, still chewing (click).

'Nothing, hon. I'm just tired!' I said, wishing to God she wouldn't talk with her mouth full.

Three is never a good number. Whenever someone tried to play with me and Sarah, it never worked out. Marie Johnston played with us at school for a while, but she went to Sarah's house once, and it didn't go well. Their parents had a big falling-out, apparently. Marie didn't come to school the next day, and by the time she returned a week later, she said she didn't want to play with us anymore.

After lunch, as we practically crawled along the loch-side path, I started to feel bored and annoyed with Sarah's whingeing, and a distinct desire to play with number three. So after five miles, I stopped stopping every time Sarah did. And after ten miles, Kyle stopped stopping every time Sarah did. And after fifteen miles, we stopped taking a break every now and again so Sarah could catch up, and stopped asking her if her feet were any better. Instead, we walked together, fast, almost running, inspired by each other's energy, practically laughing with exhilaration, pushing through branches and up rocky ridges, one foot and then the next.

Endorphins must have been flooding my veins because I felt like I was flying when I reached Inverarnan. Kyle and I did a high five in front of the old pub. Sitting down with a cold beer, we started feeling more and more guilty about our treatment of Sarah. She wasn't as fit as us, after all.

Chastened, we went and booked two rooms in the quirky old pub as a treat for Sarah because today was her eighth wedding anniversary and Kyle had totally forgotten until now.

16

The day along Loch Lomond was excruciating for Sarah. Her feet had blistered on both balls and heels. For the first ten miles, she stopped and put new plasters on each of the four pressure points, but then she ran out of plasters and her feet became too slippery with blood to hold them, so she merely stopped to assess the damage. Krissie and Kyle were too far ahead now and she was ashamed to ask some German walkers to get them. Why her feet? Why, out of all six possible feet, did her two have to be the ones that couldn't cope with this endless path full of endless branches?

As she scrambled over branches and up rocky paths she made herself count to ten, breathe deeply, keep walking.

The techniques she'd learned at therapy were quite useful, as it turned out. She could tune out, and cope. But when you have to tune out continuously because your feet have been ripped to shreds and your husband and best friend have abandoned you — on your wedding anniversary — you start counting to ten through your teeth, and you start breathing fast and deep through your nose. And eventually, you start sobbing and then chanting a chant that goes like this: 'That fucking bastard! Those fucking bastards. Bastards!'

They always left her out when they were together. They shared a past, having lived together during their college years. Even now they seemed to have an intuitive understanding of each other and know things Sarah didn't which they loved reminiscing about. Kyle smoked dope with Chas. They'd bagged two Munros (i.e. walked up two big hills for no good reason) together. They'd had a friend at uni called Bridget. They loved spicy sausage pasta.

It also surprised and angered her when they seemed to have read the same newspaper articles on the latest war or on the opposition leadership race or on that new arthouse director and talked interminably about said issues.

Sarah had been thinking such things as she took her rucksack off in front of the pub.

'Surprise!' Krissie and Kyle yelled from an upstairs window.

Having thought bad thoughts about them for several hours, it was hard to be pleased when they showed her to her quaint room, poured her a glass of champagne and ushered her towards a huge bath filled with salts and bubbles. It took several minutes in the tub with the lights low to stop hating them more than life itself, and to start loving them again. Her husband of eight years and her friend since forever.

When Sarah came down to dinner she was prepared for a fantastic meal and ready to enjoy herself.

But after the starter of prawn cocktail and one glass of Australian cabernet sauvignon, her feelings of hatred re-emerged. Would they ever stop talking about university? What was so interesting about that Chas guy with the greasy hair and large pupils?

Before she knew it, she'd eaten her pudding and was saying, 'That was lovely, thanks, but I'm exhausted. I think I'll hit the sack.'

Kyle did the right thing — she had to give him that — he offered to come with her three times or more. But she refused . . . 'No, no, you guys stay, I'll see you in the morning.'

She lay in her bed fuming for the next four hours. How could Kyle have let her go to bed by herself on their anniversary? Having sex on your anniversary is a duty, and under no circumstances should it be overlooked.

Eventually, she got dressed in a fury and went downstairs. To her surprise, there was no-one in the living room, and no-one in the bar. All was deadly quiet.

She looked out the window into the garden — nothing but darkness.

Then, from nowhere, Matt's face appeared behind the glass. Sarah jumped back and watched as Matt turned and walked towards his tent.

Her heart eventually slowed down again, and she returned to the task at hand. Where were they? Where could they have gone?

But she knew really. It was obvious where they were.

Sarah didn't breathe at all as she walked up the stairs. It seemed like hours had gone by when she finally reached the first floor. She gulped as she drifted along the corridor towards Krissie's room.

She paused, turned the handle slowly.

Opened the door slowly.

Walked towards the bed slowly.

Turned on the light fast.

But there was no-one there. Funny how it felt almost disappointing. Over the last four hours Sarah had fantasised about catching them at it, had planned the self-righteous walk out the door, envisaged the sale of the houses and the permanent move to France and the nice thirty-year-old neighbour called Jean-Luc who would give her armfuls of home-grown aubergines and then several babies.

Now none of this was going to happen and it was disappointing.

Sarah's therapist had explained this kind of thinking to her because she did it a lot. If Kyle was late from work she would worry herself into a frenzy and imagine him dead on the side of the road or murdered in an underground car park. Ms Therapist had said that this thinking was not due to worry, but anger. When Kyle was late, it made her feel better to imagine that his throat was cut or that he had been sodomised to the point of rupture by an escaped convict. It was anger and it was not healthy — remember the techniques?

So Sarah went back down to the living room and counted to ten and breathed deeply for what seemed like forever.

Just as Sarah's heart rate came back down to earth, Krissie and Kyle giggled their way into the foyer, covered in mud. Seeing her, their carefree expressions turned to naughty-schoolchildren expressions.

'Sarah!' said Kyle.

'Matt's out there! Do you think he's a serial killer?' asked Krissie. 'He has on the same clothes — those same khaki shorts — and his hands are huge!'

'Look what we found!' said Kyle.

They showed her a bag of dirty mush-rooms.

'Let's do it!' said Kyle.

'What?' asked Sarah, as she took the bag from Krissie to have a look.

'Magic mushrooms! They're everywhere!'

What followed was an argument, which can be summarised thus:

Sarah: 'So how old are you exactly?'

Kyle: Rolls eyes.

Krissie: Gives Kyle a knowing smile.

Sarah: Notes exchange, throws bag of mushrooms at Kyle, shouts, 'Get fucked the both of you,' and hobbles upstairs.

While fuming in bed, Sarah went over the usual cringe-worthy analysis of her cutting retort. 'Get fucked' couldn't begin to convey the extent and complexity of her grievances. She actually couldn't believe that's all she had said, and that no-one had followed her upstairs to beg her forgiveness. It was as if she didn't exist. If things didn't get better tomorrow, she decided, she would leave. Leave this stupid holiday, leave Kyle, leave Scotland. Perhaps, she thought, as she sometimes did, she would even leave the world.

She was so tired from crying that she fell asleep and didn't hear Kyle come in. Instead, she woke to a strangely wonderful sensation and after a moment of semi-conscious bliss she realised that Kyle was licking her where he had never licked her before. She was horrified at what was happening, and walloped him over the head.

'Yuck! What are you doing? What is wrong with you? Have you taken those mushrooms?'

'No!' Kyle surfaced, rubbing his skull. 'I just thought, something different.'

'You thought 'something different'! Jesus Christ, Kyle, you ignore me all night on our anniversary, and then — yuck! Clean your teeth!'

Kyle did as he was told and then fell asleep.

★　★　★

Over breakfast the next morning, Krissie and Kyle giggled like lunatics as the pedantic hotelier rearranged all the knick-knacks on shelves and mantles and hearths and sills.

Why were they laughing? wondered Sarah. Were they laughing at her? What little secrets were they sharing? What was so damn funny about the knick-knacks on the window sills?

As much as she wanted to scream, Sarah ate calmly. She was giving it one more day. She would be reasonable and logical, and she would try to salvage the holiday.

17

It makes it worse somehow that I fell for Kyle on the night of his wedding anniversary. I don't think I'd ever properly fallen in love before, because I had never experienced the physical discomfort of it. It felt the same as grieving — intense, agonising, all-consuming. Why would falling in love feel the same as grief? I suddenly couldn't eat. It felt like I could hardly breathe.

That night with Kyle felt like it was the most wonderful night of my life. I found myself looking him directly in the eyes for longer than is socially acceptable. I noticed him noticing my bare arms and liking what he saw. I felt his body warm me like a heater even though he was several feet away. I knew he wanted to be closer. I touched his hand accidentally when I handed him a glass of wine and his hand lingered near mine several times after.

Kyle and I drank till the wee hours, rearranged the incredible number of ornaments in the dining room, collected magic mushrooms, and then dared each other to walk into the woods and stand still for five minutes in the pitch-black. I lasted one minute. Kyle lasted six. I thought he might be dead, so I started to walk towards the black trees to find him.

I heard a noise that put my post-pregnancy pelvic floor muscles to the test, turned around, and saw Matt in the distance, peering through a window into the hotel and then walking towards the field. I kept deadly still, but Kyle 'booed' me from behind, which made Matt turn around. I looked at Matt for a full four seconds — doesn't sound long, but when you're looking at someone who might want to rape and kill you it's (cat dog) . . . a (cat dog) . . . long (cat dog) . . . time (cat dog).

I grabbed Kyle and ran with him back to the hotel, and we slammed the door shut and locked it with painstaking drunkenness. When we turned around, Sarah was there, and she scared us almost as much as Matt had. She looked mad — and was mad, as it turned out; so mad, in fact, that it took us ages to collect all the magic mushrooms she hurled across the foyer floor before turning on her heel and stomping off.

If Kyle follows her upstairs, I told myself, then I'm imagining things. If he stays, that's it, I'm in trouble. We're all in trouble.

A pause.

'There's some of that port left,' said Kyle.

So that was it, we were in trouble.

We sat in the bar together and talked.

Topics covered: favourite song, what we would study if we had our time again, how I'd been feeling since the bub, how Kyle was coping with the pressure of his work and marriage.

How could it be that I'd suddenly fallen for a guy I'd known for years? How could it be that I hadn't noticed how good he made me feel about myself? I just knew he liked me, and that he enjoyed my company.

I'd started to sober up a little when our talk turned (dangerously) to what unusual sexual experiences we had had. Turns out Kyle had quite a limited repertoire, so I sent him off to bed to try something new, and sat there by myself regretting it.

★　★　★

The next morning I was up first, after a two-hour headachy sleep. Matt's tent was gone from the field, just like last time. I sat and ate breakfast by myself, jumping every time I heard a noise that might be Kyle — footsteps, a door opening, voices.

He finally appeared during my third coffee. What a weird thing. The day before I was unaware of the hairs on my arms, I knew how to go about eating food, and I was able to put two or more words together in order to convey information. What had happened to me? My arm hairs were fully erect. My skin had flu-like tingles all over. I could only breathe in as far as my tonsils. And I had regressed to the speaking age of a toddler.

Mind you, I must have managed to say something while we drank our coffee, because I remember wishing Sarah hadn't interrupted our conversation. She sat down to eat her fry-up and apologised for the night before. She was sorry. She'd just been tired. Today she would try really hard. She was determined to keep up with us and her feet were well bandaged and feeling fine.

We headed off towards Bridge of Orchy, leaving Loch Lomond behind us and venturing into bleakness. Sarah didn't complain at all but she lagged behind a bit, and when she caught up with us at our first break she seemed to be walking barefoot.

'My God, Sarah, what's happened?' I asked her, as she sat down beside me. Her feet were bleeding, and skin was hanging off where blisters had popped.

'It's the new walking shoes, I think,' she said. 'Do you mind if I hitch a ride to the campsite?'

We both protested. How about we all hitch a ride? We couldn't let her go off alone.

But she insisted, and seemed fine about it, promising to have a fire roaring for us at the campsite.

So we walked past a huge old deserted quarry and then waited with her beside a small road in the middle of nowhere until a car came along — a Sainsbury's delivery van to be precise. Before she got in I asked the driver if he was an axe murderer. He shook his head: 'I prefer to use a shotgun.' Sarah hopped into the seat beside him and smiled.

As the van disappeared into the distance, a wave of panic tingled through me. For miles and miles, there would be nothing and no-one but the two of us.

I don't think I moved for a few seconds. I was too scared to. If I looked at Kyle, that would be it. So instead I formulated Plan A in my brain, which involved walking quickly, eyes down, and talking non-stop about safe, non-flirtatious topics.

'It's hard to believe, isn't it, how Chas turned out,' I said, almost jogging, eyes determinedly down.

'Remember how he used to feed the ants under the sink? With caramel shortcake, the classy bastard. Best-fed ants in Glasgow!'

'He is the nicest man I've ever known,' I said.

'Nicer than me?' said Kyle, looking into my eyes.

Shite. What was Plan B? I didn't have one. Shite.

'Of course he is!' I said. 'You're a pain in the arse.'

18

Just about the time Krissie and Kyle were waving goodbye to Sarah, their old friend Chas was sitting on the top bunk in his cell, holding his full supermarket bag, waiting.

The knock eventually came at one-thirty, just at the end of *Neighbours*. Although he'd been anticipating it all day — for every day of his sentence, in actual fact — when it came it scared the hell out of him.

Four years he'd spent in that cell in B Hall. Forty-eight months. Two hundred and eight weeks. One thousand, four hundred and sixty-one days. His crime had been to attack a man with a metal bar that he'd managed to dislodge from a trolley. His reason for doing it hadn't come out during the trial.

When Chas was being sentenced at the Old Bailey, the judge had looked him in the eye and asked him if he felt any remorse for what he had done.

Chas had held the judge's gaze and replied, 'No'.

If the judge was to look Chas in the eye now and ask him if he was sorry for what he'd done, if he was sorry that one thousand, four hundred and sixty-one days of his life had been spent in this hellhole because of what he had done, Chas would look him in the eye again and answer exactly the same. He would say no. He felt no remorse. None whatsoever.

Chas thought back now to his fear when he'd first heard his sentence and which prison he'd be going to. It had almost been a relief to be transferred to Sandhill, even though he'd heard about Sandhill's hard men and was properly scared to death when he was taken north in a white van. A man in a uniform handcuffed him and took him through the metal door and then into Reception, where he was processed.

He saw pretty much straight away that he wouldn't fit into either camp of prisoner at Sandhill. There were the criers, who were shocked to find themselves where they were, who had lost houses or jobs or wives because of where they were, and who sobbed uncontrollably for weeks. Then there were the 'hiya-big-fella' guys, who arrived as if they were at a school reunion — chatting to old mates in what must have felt a familiar, almost safe, place.

Chas was in a third category all of his own. No regulation scar on the face, no glint in the eye, no drugs to sell or buy, no loss of family or job. He was the spacey middle-class guy. A little bit scrawny, but otherwise good-looking, well dressed and highly articulate. Chas recognised immediately that he would need to keep a low profile and hide his differences. So he'd put his head down, painted, refused to see visitors, and barely spoke to anyone for four years.

He'd been 'dubbed' up with five different men over his time there — a smoker who meowed and didn't do it; an injector who did and would again; two men with mad-bitch wives who drove them to it; and young Kieran, who cried for the entirety of his eighty-day lie-down.

★　★　★

Chas changed into the white overalls the boss gave him, and held tight onto his bag as he followed him out of the hall. He thought he'd feel more as the keys dangled and the huge metal doors opened, but he didn't feel much at all. The boss he liked had said goodbye the night before, and no-one else gave a damn about him.

The most important thing Chas had learnt in prison was from a ten-minute conversation with a nurse. He'd asked to see one, just because it was one of the few things that you could choose to do in prison. This girl came to see him, and listened to him rant about how he had failed to look after the person he loved. That was why he was in here, for trying to look after the person he loved. But he had failed.

The nurse told him that he should stop blaming himself. He had tried his best and it wasn't his fault. Instead, he should look after himself. He should let himself be loved.

Chas was dumbfounded. She was right. It had not been his fault and he did deserve to be loved. As the door locked Chas in again, he looked at the silver-white cell and knew who it was who should love him. It was Krissie.

As the taxi took Chas into town, he felt like he was on a rollercoaster — out of control, on the brink of death. Too much noise, too much speed, too many people. He put his hands over his ears and only lifted his eyes when the taxi driver shook him on the leg. 'That's you.'

Chas stepped out of the taxi and looked at the house in front of him. It was a nice wee terraced house in a nice wee suburb of Glasgow. He took a deep breath, checked his hair in the side mirror of a parked car, and walked up to the door.

Krissie's dad, Dave, answered the door

holding a crying baby boy and looking a little bit frazzled.

'Chas! How are you? Are you okay? Come in! It's so nice to see you. Anna's just gone out to get Calpol for Robbie here, she'll just be a sec. Come away in.'

'No, no, I won't. I was just wondering if Krissie's about.'

'She's on holiday, camping. We're minding the wee one. This is Robbie, Krissie's son.'

Chas's heart sank at the realisation that Krissie had hooked up with someone, but he did his best to hide it.

'Oh, hello, Robbie! You've got your mummy's eye-lashes, haven't you? So where have your mummy and daddy gone?'

'His mummy is away with Kyle and Sarah.'

'Oh, and Robbie's daddy?'

Dave shook his head. 'He's not around. It's a long story. Krissie'll be back in a few days. Here's her number . . . She's still in Gardner Street. But listen, come in and wait for Anna. She'll be sad if she misses you. And you're welcome to stay with us until you get back on your feet.'

'Thanks, but Mum and Dad have already ironed my Hibs duvet!'

But before Chas could head off to his parents Krissie's mum arrived. She dropped her shopping bags at the front gate when she saw who was at the door. 'Chas!' she said, running to give him a hug.

Anna used to bring packets of food to the flat Chas shared with Krissie and Kyle — fantastic meatballs and cakes and even the odd bottle of wine. Chas had adored her — she always seemed to say the right thing if he was having a difficult time. She oozed happiness, had a wonderfully elegant face and was an amateur philosopher. She loved nothing better than to sip coffee in the bay window, people-watching, and making observations like: 'You know, Chas, I think there's only so much happiness for each person. Like half a glass maybe, and you just can't expect more. So what's a person to do, sip or skol?'

Chas knew when he met Krissie's mum that Krissie was only going to get better with age. She was like a good cabernet, softening and smoothing with time.

'Come back in,' Anna insisted, taking him by the arm and not giving him the opportunity to object. While Anna poured tea, Chas stood at the kitchen bench, marvelling at the abnormality of normality. The very act of placing eight custard creams on a plate seemed surreal to him.

'It's hard to explain,' he said, when Anna asked him what his time had been like. 'I guess it's like being on an aeroplane with drunk football fans for four years ... on Aeroflot!'

Dave gave Robbie some Calpol and then rocked him to sleep in his arms.

This was more comfortable to Chas than anywhere else in the world. Certainly it was more comfortable than his parents' home, with its stiff antique furniture and tastefully appointed bedrooms (bar the Hibs duvet). This was the kind of home Chas had always wanted.

There were silences as they skirted around issues — none of them wanting to talk about assaults or postnatal depression — but they were the kind of silences families have, not comfortable so much as just not uncomfortable; the kind where everyone knows everything there is to know.

As Chas left, Anna hugged him firmly. There was a tear in her eye as Chas smiled and walked off.

As he walked past the row of terraces, Chas felt like flying with happiness. She wasn't married. She was alone. And he was going to find her.

19

In the Sainsbury's delivery van, Sarah chatted happily to her shotgun killer. It had been quite some time since she'd had the old effect on men, and it was very clear that it was happening now. She was still blonde, still had huge boobs and white teeth, and could still flutter her eyebrows and giggle girlishly.

Paul was about forty, and it turned out that he was the manager of all the Sainsbury's stores in the Highlands. Every so often, he explained, he spent a day in the life of one of his workers, so he could keep in touch. He lived in a castle near Perth, and spent his evenings drinking champagne and his weekends horse-riding and showing the kids a good time.

Sarah immediately felt she could trust Paul. There was something about him, something that saw the real her, understood the real her, and it was truly liberating to be listened to and respected.

'What about you?' he asked Sarah. 'What's your life like?'

Before Sarah knew it, she was crying. Her life, actually, was shit. She was lonely and her marriage was at breaking point. Her husband clearly preferred the company of her best friend. She felt fat and frumpy. Paul tutted and told her she was beautiful, that he didn't understand the attraction of rake-thin women. It seemed no time at all before Paul stopped the van at the campsite, where he insisted on setting up the tent while she had a shower and bandaged her feet.

'Feel like a beer?' Paul asked after she returned from the shower.

They sat in the local pub and talked. Paul's marriage had ended several years earlier. His wife, he confided, had left him in the end after hundreds of ultimatums about working less and spending more time kicking the football around with the kids. He didn't listen, and she made good on her threats.

It was eight p.m. when Sarah next looked at the time. She was drunk, and so was Paul, and the pub had filled sufficiently with noise and smoke and people for Paul to try and kiss her. She almost let him, but decided not to.

'Not just now,' she said, tapping on the beer mat with his phone number on it.

★　★　★

While Sarah had spent a wonderful day being listened to and reassured by Paul, Krissie and

133

Kyle had walked as fast as they could to stop their adrenalin from being channelled into the wrong organs. They sped along the valleys, determined not to be distracted.

Krissie's resolve had diminished along with the miles, and there were several moments in particular that had pushed them towards lunch.

First was the derelict house. It stood in the wilderness with stone walls and no roof, its five grassy windows lined up like a train. It was an unmissable photo opportunity.

'Say 'KYLE'S GORGEOUS!'' Kyle had said as he pointed the camera.

'Kyle's gorgeous,' Krissie said, trying not to mean it.

Another moment involved a steep hill that Krissie climbed ahead of Kyle, knowing full well that her upper thighs and new red knickers would be partly visible under her loose short shorts.

Then there was the tree trunk that crossed the path. 'Here,' Kyle had said, extending a hand. Krissie had taken it in hers, jumped down beside him and not let go for the count of three, she reckoned, as she recalled it with pleasure over the next leg of the journey.

These moments were the entree moments that led to the ham roll of lunch. They sat on the top of a small hill and overlooked the grey-brown cragginess of the surrounds. They laboured through the shared roll, passing it back and forth more often than necessary. They could both hear the inner workings of mouth and throat and neither of them could finish.

'I'm not hungry,' Kyle said, as Krissie offered him another bite.

'Me neither.'

'How about these?' Kyle took the magic mushrooms out of his pocket. They were wrapped in a hotel napkin.

'No way!' said Krissie.

'I thought we could partake. Take a bite,' said Kyle.

'Do I just eat it raw? What will it do to me?'

'Give you insights.'

'Is that all?'

'Maybe make you horny.'

'Then it's not a good idea, is it?'

'So why did you just take a bite, Krissie?'

20

I'd done ecstasy in Tenerife, but never ever had I experienced anything quite like those mushrooms. Kyle and I sat on the hill and chewed, and then lay down and waited. We looked into the sky and every now and again said: 'Nup, nothing. You?'

Looking back now I know we weren't waiting for the hallucinations, we were waiting for something to open the gates and let us finish what we had already started.

About an hour later, the gates opened. But instead of making us horny, it made us see amazing truths, which flooded the hills and the rocks and our heads.

'One of us will die first and the other will have to go to the funeral.'

'Sarah is the most beautiful, giving person I have ever ever known. She looks after me. Looks. After. Me.'

'Being a doctor sucks.'

'I love you, Kyle.'

'I love you, Krissie.'

'That cloud looks like a giraffe.'

'Let's follow it.'

And so for the next hour or so Kyle and I

talked absolute shite, stopping occasionally to cry, occasionally to laugh, and eventually staggered into the campsite at about 11 p.m. How we actually found our way there I'll never know.

I was too far gone to erect my tent, so we both crawled in beside Sarah, who was sleeping like a log.

We fell asleep immediately.

When I woke up I had no idea where I was or even who I was. As my eyes adjusted, I saw Kyle lying next to me, Sarah on the other side. His face was so pretty, and I wanted to cry with love for him. And before I knew it, a desperate need overwhelmed me. I had to have him in my mouth.

I didn't give myself time to think, and slowly crawled under the covers and kissed him.

I used to have dreams about fellatio. Invariably the dicks were thin and pencil-like and — at least twice — turned to shit in my mouth, which made me wake up dry-retching. I'd thought once that these dreams meant I was a lesbian, but whenever I imagined being with a woman I worried about the logistics, and I decided that maybe the dreams just meant that I didn't much like giving head.

Nothing could have been further from the

truth that night. I could have spent my life down there. And I'll never forget the best thing about it, which was when Kyle woke with a small moan, lifted up the sleeping bag, and looked down. He locked eyes with me for a split second before he twitched in climax.

After that, Kyle and I lay in the tent and stared at each other, fully awake, all night. We were in love; desperately, passionately in love.

★   ★   ★

The next morning we cooked baked beans over the gas stove and a battle raged within me. When I was young, I called my internal arguments my 'talkers'. They would argue like this:

Don't steal the sweetie, it's wrong.

But I want it.

But it's wrong.

But it's a Curly Wurly.

You'll go to hell! Don't take it! It's wrong.

It's just chocolate. It's just a Curly Wurly.

And now here they were again, my talkers, yapping away:

It's wrong.

It's fate.

It's evil.

It's love.

Sarah to my left, Kyle to my right.

Guilt. Desire.

It was like my two fists were clenched and locked in a battle against each other — punching away before me — and while they were bashing at each other I could not eat baked beans or even drink coffee. I was immobilised and it made me angry because, in a battle like this, one thing is certain: guilt has to win. It might take a while, and it might twist and turn, but until guilt wins, there will be hell to pay.

And that made me angry.

The way I dealt with it was to walk as fast as my talkers:

The marriage is over anyway.

I won't tell her.

I'll go home. I have to go home.

How can I have done that?

Just one kiss.

What harm would one kiss . . .

Sarah doesn't understand him. The marriage has been over for years.

'Are you okay?' asked Sarah.

'Yeah, yeah, fine . . . But I can't face a tent tonight, and I need a bath.'

★　★　★

We reached the Kingshouse Hotel near Glencoe at four that afternoon. It was a shorter day, and Sarah's feet seemed to cope with it. I determined to forget the thing with Kyle, then everything would be fine, just as it was before.

That was the plan.

What happened instead was this: Sarah grabbed a trolley and took the luggage upstairs while Kyle and I sat in the bar and drank two glasses of red wine each without speaking a word.

I could tell as I looked at Kyle that he was gagging for it. He couldn't stop jigging his knee up and down, up and down, and his nerves hit the bar and ricocheted along and down to my stool.

'Kyle, what happened last night . . . ' I started.

Before I could finish he said: 'It's over between Sarah and me.'

I skolled another glass of wine and thought of all the things I liked about Kyle. He was kind, for example.

'I can't leave her, though, Krissie — she'd die.'

'I don't want you to,' I said.

After we ordered a second bottle I thought about how funny he was.

Another glass later I noticed that Kyle's thighs (he had shorts on) were coated with soft, even, light brown hair and thought about the fact that the thighs were attached to the cock I had sucked on the evening before.

I loved him, wanted him, and he saw this in my eyes and touched my knee with his hand as he reached for his wallet to pay for what was now our third bottle of wine.

When Sarah finally came downstairs in skirt and top she had clearly had a bath or shower and styled her hair. She sat carefully on a stool next to me, no doubt to avoid hair displacement, and crossed her shiny buffed legs.

'You're hammered!' she said as we laughed wildly at something not very funny.

We ate steak pie and the like and started watching Germany v England on the telly. It was an extremely important qualifying match, and the place was filled with an equal number of Germans and Scots, and a few Aussies and English. When England scored, there was light applause and the Germans looked bewildered. This was Britain. Why was the place not erupting? Then the Germans scored and the place exploded.

Bloody Scotland, I thought to myself, the alcohol having touched a less jolly part of my thinking. 'What the hell are we doing in a country that derives its only pleasure from the failure of its neighbour?'

Kyle understood, and discussed it with me

through sticky toffee pudding, but Sarah found the whole atmosphere boring and a bit depressing, and went back to her room — again.

We danced to the eighties tunes on offer with the (victorious) Germans. Kyle was always a dad dancer — white man's overbite, finger clicking, the occasional inappropriate twirl — but he made me laugh and was agile enough to catch me when I copied his twirl and almost fell to the ground. As he scooped me up, we noticed Matt and his evil eye at the bar. He had his arm around the pretty blonde girl who'd served us our pie and I noticed a tattoo on his upper arm. LOVE, it said. Most fitting, and original.

'Let me take you to your room,' said Kyle, putting his arm around my waist. We staggered upstairs and along the corridor.

The hotel was two hundred years old, painted white, and on three levels. There were about forty rooms, and in our highly intoxicated state it took us a while to find mine. I fell to my bed with a clunk and Kyle stood over me, wondering.

'Sit here for a bit!' I banged on the bed beside me, and Kyle did as he was told, sitting down next to my horizontal swirling body.

'So did you do something rude and

imaginative with Sarah the other night?' I asked.

'I tried, but she wasn't into it.'

'What did you do?'

'Not telling.'

'Go on!' I said, tickling the thigh that had so enthralled me all evening. '*Show* me then.'

'I don't want to do rude and imaginative with you, Krissie,' he said, and then lay down beside me, looking deep into my eyes and stroking my hair. 'I want to do nice and tender.'

With this, he kissed me, and I could see what he was aiming for. A soft meaningful kiss that takes your breath away. But I was way too drunk for nice, so for a while we fought each other — me wanting fast/aggressive/over-soon-please-as-I-may-well-puke — him wanting slow/loving/meaningful.

By the time we got past the lengthy foreplay period, I had decided that it was best to go missionary because I had found a spot on the ceiling that, if I focused on it very hard, would stop the spinning.

I lay back and stared at it while Kyle undertook a rather adolescent thrusting, which he paused every few seconds in an agonising attempt to prevent ejaculation. He closed his eyes and grimaced as he throbbed.

'I don't mind!' I said to him, hoping to

God he'd just let it happen, but he was obviously devastated by his performance and didn't.

'No, no, it's okay, just a minute!' he kept saying. 'I can . . . I can hold off . . . just . . . '

'JUST COME FOR GOD'S SAKE!' a voice yelled.

I looked at Kyle's scrunched-up eyes, which opened in horror at the statement, and the throb stopped because he'd lost concentration and therefore control. Still on top of me, he stared into my eyes and then turned his head ninety degrees to the left and saw Sarah standing beside him.

'Thank God for that, Kyle, the girl was about to throw up!' she said, her voice flat but with an edge that plummeted into dark, scary territory.

We jumped, took cover, did all the things they do in the movies.

But Sarah played her role all wrong. She didn't hit us or shoot us or yell or slam the door or even leave. Dressed only in her silk chemise, she sat down softly on the end of the bed and started to speak with a primary school teacher's voice and no sign of a quivering lip.

'It's okay, don't worry. This can be sorted out. All we have to do is be logical.'

From me: 'Sarah! I'm so sorry!'

From Kyle: 'I didn't want to hurt you. I never meant for this to happen.'

'You're not listening, are you? I'm not angry. We can sort this out. Krissie, you and I have each got something that the other wants.'

'What are you talking about?'

'You can have each other. I don't mind.'

Kyle and I looked perplexed.

'What do you mean?' I asked.

'You can have each other, but there's a condition.'

I stared at her.

She smiled, almost kindly. 'I get Robbie.'

I was so shocked I couldn't move.

Then my shock turned to anger. I didn't care that I was naked under a threadbare sheet with Sarah's husband. I was furious. I got out of bed and began to dress.

'You're fucking crazy!' I said.

I pulled my pants on in full view of both of them. Zipped up my jeans. Tied shoelaces. Put difficult-to-untangle sports bra on, then T-shirt. I stuffed all my things into my rucksack and strapped my tent to it. It took ages and was awkward and I was amazed that Sarah and Kyle continued to watch me the entire time, but they did, both sitting on the bed, watching until I walked out the door.

Sarah followed me to the foyer, where Matt

and his pretty waitress were snogging on the abandoned dance floor. Like teenagers, their mouths moved angrily without pause.

'Where are you going?' Sarah yelled.

Matt and his bird stopped for air.

'How dare you, Sarah?'

'I hardly think *you* should be indignant. You left Robbie alone in your flat screaming while you screwed that ned downstairs. And you just fucked my husband.'

Matt and his bird sniggered into each other's shoulders, and then resumed the eating.

I rushed out of the foyer and slammed the door. The cold night air hit me head on and I began to walk. I didn't know where to, didn't care. I just had to get away. From Sarah. From Kyle. From what I had just done. From what I was. A dreadful person.

And Sarah was right. I was an appalling mother.

My walk became a run as I sped upwards along a trail. The light of the hotel was replaced by moonshine, which was enough for me to see that the path had become thinner and more difficult, that it was twisting up a ridge, getting steeper and steeper. I staggered over rocks, losing the path, and climbed and climbed in the blackness, crawling, in the end, to escape.

21

I must have been walking for about an hour, because eventually I reached the top of a hill and lay on my back breathing fast and shaking. Was I such a bad person that Sarah could honestly think I'd just hand Robbie over, like that? I was, wasn't I? I was a bad person, and I should be punished.

I held my hands over my eyes to stop the stars from swirling, and when I took my hands away, I screamed, because Sarah, dressed in her silk nightie and Gore-tex jacket, was standing over me.

She held out her hand and hauled me to my feet and then grabbed my arm so tightly that it hurt. This was very scary. I had never had a fistfight with anyone, let alone my best friend since forever. I had never even wanted to. I was an only child with parents who loved each other and rarely yelled, so aggression and violence were alien to me.

The pain in my arm was piercing and I was in shock, unsure how to react. I imagined, as I found my way upright, that I would apologise for the unforgivable thing I'd just done, and that she would make me pay with a look that penetrated the depths of my Catholic soul. But also that somehow, through time, we might get over it. Wrong.

'How dare you play hard done by? You're a slut and you don't deserve your child,' she screamed at me.

'What?'

'You're the worst mother I've ever known, and you're a whore.'

'Sarah!'

'After all I've done for you! I've dedicated myself to you. Ever since that time when we were little, I've watched out for you, and this is what I get, you ungrateful deceitful SLUT.'

'What time when we were little?'

'Don't pretend you don't remember,' Sarah yelled.

The air coming out of her nose was noisy, and her lips were crinkle-cut blue from the pursing. She moved towards me and I was petrified. What was she going to do? Punch me? Surely not.

Yes. She was going to punch me. She crunched her manicured fist into a tiny little ball and moved her elbow back expertly as if she were aiming her bow and arrow.

I cowered behind my hands like a baby while she punched me again and again on the top of my head. It went on and on. It was never going to stop. I was going to be punched on the top of the head until I disappeared into the cliff like a nail.

I removed my hands from my face and took one on the chin in the interim.

'You do remember! You're a liar! Since then I promised myself I'd never let anything bad happen to you, and this is the thanks I get,' Sarah yelled, hitting me in the face again.

I pushed her away with as much heave-ho as I could muster. I don't remember seeing what happened when I did this, because I had shut my eyes with the shame of it. All I know is that when the push was over I opened my eyes and Sarah wasn't there.

I shook my head and closed my eyes tight, and then opened them again slowly. I was still there, on the edge of a cliff with a sore head and no Sarah.

'Sarah?'

Nothing.

'Sarah!'

I spun around to see if she was behind me, with her squirrel's fist ready to go at me again, or if she was hiding in the shadow of the boulder beside me, waiting. I crept around in the darkness at the top of that cliff, scouring the area, but she was nowhere to be seen.

Still terrified that she might pounce on me suddenly, I yelled again. 'SARAH! I'M

SORRY, PLEASE COME OUT! PLEASE! I'M SO SORRY!'

She didn't answer and I began to panic. I made the sign of the cross that please God, please God, I hadn't done her any harm. I scrabbled around trying to find her in the bushes, hoping she'd headed back to Kyle. Then I bent over the edge and looked down.

The moon and the stars were bright enough for me to see that the cliff face was practically vertical . . .

. . . and there was a body lying at the bottom of it.

Knowing there was no time to get help, I searched the cliff edge and found a ridge gradual enough to climb down. Focusing on each step, one at a time, I eventually reached the bottom. I then ran along the base towards the bent lump I'd seen from the top. She could be alive, I told myself. She could be okay.

But she wasn't. When I found her she was face down in heather. Turning her over, I screamed and screamed.

Her eyes were closed and I knew she was dead.

I screamed again, and cried and shook and punched things and jumped up and down on the spot and cried again and then sat with my face in my hands, trembling. And when I took my hands away from my face I saw that they were drenched in blood. I fainted, and when I came to, her body was still lifeless.

'God, God, Sarah, I'm sorry. What have I done? Oh no, God, I'm sorry. Please please please help! HELP ME!'

Some common sense must have returned because I tried to phone 999. I ran up and down hills and perched myself on precipices trying to get reception, finally managing to get a couple of notches. Then the screen lit up and I saw Robbie's picture. I'd taken the photo the same day I'd shagged Marco. It was the first day of my good-mother strategy. I was going to hang out with Robbie for long periods of time, play with him on living room floors, make Santa beards in bubble baths and don clever voices at story-time. I had resolved to be a selfless, constant mother. As I looked at the picture of my baby snoozing in his buggy by the duck pond, his little face melted me. He needed me. I couldn't phone the police. I would lose him.

It was almost as if I'd flicked a switch as the realisation hit me and I returned to logical mode. What options did I have? Run away and leave Sarah's body where it was? Bury her somewhere? Go back and tell Kyle and see what he thought I should do?

I looked at Robbie's face again. There were

no choices. I had to hide her.

I saw how high and remote I was. It felt like I was in the middle of nowhere, enveloped by inhospitable treeless mountains. I headed back towards Sarah's body and started to descend. There were caves and crevices in the cliff face, and when the slope became more gentle I began searching for an opening that might do. It took a while — most of them were too big, too small or too high — but eventually I found one that was just right. It was about thirty metres from the ridge I'd climbed down and almost impossible to see from below, let alone above. The front of it was covered in blue-green heather and it was only when you pushed the brush away that you noticed the opening. It was perfect.

I walked across to where Sarah was lying, touched her hair with my hand, and started crying. Sarah. My best friend since we were little girls. Murdered by me.

I clambered back up to where I'd left my rucksack, and retrieved the tent. I threw it down, blanching when it landed on Sarah's body. Shit! (Too hard to think about now, I told myself.)

I raced back down again, my head throbbing from a mixture of hangover, exertion and Sarah's punches, and then laid the tent out flat on the ground at the foot of the crevice. I took the pegs out and threw them aside, zipped Sarah's jacket over her flimsy nightwear then began to move my best friend's body from the heather onto the purple Gore-tex.

Nothing seemed real. She was still Sarah, not a body. I sat down in shock. Then I began shaking and sobbing. I pulled myself together and wrapped Sarah like a present, rolling her over and over till the loose material surrounded her, and covered her head in a neat envelope-shape at the end.

Oh God.

It took me an eternity to lift her body up and into the crevice, but I managed. The only problem was that her left arm kept coming out of its wrapping and falling out. I'd put it back in, but it always fell out again.

Exhausted, I gave up for a while and gathered rocks to cover the opening, but when I came back to the task at hand, that arm just would not go away.

My adrenalin kicked in again when I realised it was going to get light soon. I risked being discovered by walkers who would ring the police. I thought of Robbie again, then I picked up a rock and smashed Sarah's shoulder bone. It crunched.

I shoved the dislocated arm behind Sarah's neck. It looked like it was completely separate from the tent-wrapped body, an arm by itself in a ludicrous position.

After I'd put the last rock at the mouth of the crevice, I noticed the tent pegs. One at a time, I pressed my foot onto them and pushed them into the earth.

I then climbed back up to the top of the cliff, grabbed my rucksack, forced myself to stop crying and set off back down to the hotel.

Halfway down, my legs shaking and tears streaming down my face, a group of Germans passed by. It was dawn, and the land was grey-purple with the first hint of the sun. I put my head down and tried to hide from them. They were hungover too, after the football victory of the evening before, and grunted at me without noticing my bloody face, tears, mascara stains, shakes, bruises, and no doubt evil murderous eyes. I thanked God and lifted my head again, only to find Matt standing in front of me in his trademark gear.

'Shit!' I jumped.

'Are you all right?' he asked.

'I'm fine,' I said, not looking fine at all.

'Did that prick hurt you?'

'No, no, he didn't hurt me.'

'Listen, I never meant to . . . you know, insist.'

'That's fine, Matt,' I said, walking away from him.

He yelled after me. Something about telling that guy Kyle he'd better fucking watch out. What goes around comes around, I think he said.

I ran the rest of the way.

When I reached the hotel, walkers had gathered outside with maps and thermoses ready for the hardest day of the walk, and staff inside were getting breakfast ready. I ran through the foyer and upstairs into my room.

Shutting the door behind me, I fell to the floor.

I don't know how much time passed before I crawled into the shower, the blood and tears pouring from me. Steam filled the room.

Then I heard Sarah's voice.

'Krissie! Kriss!'

I slowly pulled back the curtain. But I couldn't see a thing. Then a wave of fresh air cleared the steam a little, and her face came into view.

I screamed.

'Shit, sorry, Kriss,' said Kyle. 'I thought you were dead. I've been knocking for ages.'

I grabbed a towel.

'You have some blood on your head!'

'Oh, I fell. It's fine.'

'Is everything okay?'

'No, it's not, you know it's not!'

I started to cry and Kyle sat me on a chair and put his arm around me.

'Listen. It's been over for a long, long time. We both knew that. We haven't had sex in months. I know this is awful, but it had to happen.'

My crying was noisy but he was not put off.

'You don't understand,' I started.

'I do understand. Perfectly. I think I've loved you for years. Maybe I loved you from the first moment I laid eyes on you. Remember? You had on a black fisherman's cap.'

I reached for the half bottle of wine from the night before and emptied it down my throat.

'Can you get me some more?' I asked.

He ran off downstairs and came back up barely a minute later.

I was lying on the bed when he returned, not with the wine I'd requested, but with vodka. Sex drink.

I gulped that down and took a shaky breath. 'Sarah — ' I started.

'She'll have gone to the cottage,' he said, standing in front of me. 'She left and didn't come back last night — didn't even take her luggage. So there's nothing we can do.'

'I need to talk to you,' I said, but he hushed me with his finger and sat beside me on the bed.

'She wanted out. This trip was a last-ditch effort. My idea . . . stupid! So we shouldn't feel guilty. We should feel relieved. I feel relieved.' He put his hand against my cheek affectionately.

'Kyle, you don't understand, you have to leave.'

'No I don't.' He pushed the hair off my face.

I flicked his hand away.

'Hey,' he said, playing with my hair again. 'It's okay.'

'Kyle, stop!'

He almost fell off the bed with the force of my shove.

'Jesus!' he said, standing up.

'Just get away from me!' I yelled.

He stood and looked at me, first with bewilderment and then with enlightenment. In a whispery thin voice he said out loud: 'Derek was right. You are all the fucking same.'

22

Kyle sat in the double room next to Krissie's and cried. He wasn't sure exactly what he was crying about but there were several possibilities.

His marriage was over.

He had hurt his wife, and he hadn't meant to.

He had got carried away with one of their oldest friends.

And he was powerless to change any of the above.

Kyle had been taught very young to control his emotions. As a toddler, he spent many evenings on the second step of his family's rather large West End townhouse learning to control his emotions. As a teenager he spent long sleepless nights in his boarding school dormitory learning to control them. And as a husband he had controlled them for so long they had disappeared.

It was a relief to cry, but he did not have the comfortable facial expressions of a seasoned crier, and when he saw his reflection in the mirror, he did not like what he saw and decided to turn his attention to things that he could control. He wiped his eyes and picked up the phone . . .

'Mum, can I come and stay with you for a bit?' he said, somehow comforted by the vision of his mother on the other end of the phone — a well-dressed woman sipping a cup of tea in her rather large West End townhouse.

'Of course you can, Kyle. Is everything okay?'

'Yes, everything's fine,' Kyle replied, and she did not question him further as she, too, had secured her feelings in a lockfast place.

Both felt relieved when the conversation was over, and both stood up, sighed a quick determined sigh, and got on with the (revised) business of the day.

For Kyle's mum this involved transforming the storage-for-furniture-past-its-use-by-date room back to its original use as her only son's bedroom.

For Kyle, this was packing and leaving as fast as possible. He would not talk to Krissie again, he would apologise to his wife, but with the expectation that further discussions were likely to take place via lawyers.

Before he had packed the rucksacks (without folding anything), he was already feeling better about things. It had to happen. It was messy, but it was always going to be messy, and at least now he could get on with his life.

Sarah always used to get annoyed with Kyle for his ability to pick himself up and keep going. When they argued, she would inevitably storm out the door and he would inevitably resume reading his paper. This irritated Sarah more than anything. He should come after her, or at least sit in regretful silence for a few minutes to mourn the pleasant evening they had lost. But no, Kyle seemed to need no recovery time. He turned straight to the Letters to the Editor.

Kyle left the room without sweeping for forgotten items. He shut the door without checking again that it was definitely locked. He signed the bill without scrutinising it, and then took one of each of the newspapers on the coffee table in the foyer without wondering if he would be allowed to read them.

Kyle walked with a skip to the bus stop. He sat down on the bench and began to read the travel section of the *Herald*. Then it came to him. He could give up his job and travel. He and Sarah would sell the huge house in Glasgow and the cottage on Loch Katrine and he would take the £233,000 he estimated he'd get in the divorce and go places he'd never been before. He was so excited that he phoned his friend Derek to break the news.

'I'm going to Bulgaria!' he said. 'You were right. All women are the same and I'm going to Bul-fucking-garia. Let's celebrate, at the pub!'

'Oh mate, I would,' Derek said after a brief commiseration. 'But I promised I'd go to Homebase and get some trellis.'

Kyle hung up, a little dejected, but thought, 'Fuck it! If I can go to Bulgaria by myself then I can go to the pub by myself too.'

He was wondering what he might wear to the pub when Krissie walked towards him, looking white and unwell.

'Hi,' she said.

'Hi,' he replied, then returned to the travel article.

The two of them somehow managed to remain quiet until the bus appeared sixty seconds later.

★   ★   ★

Krissie had watched Kyle waltz out of the hotel and waited till she saw the bus coming through the valley before heading to the bus stop herself.

She had a plan, one that had come to her in the hotel room like lightning. A clear, clever and sensible plan.

She would go home, get Robbie, and hope for the best.

After all, what else could she do?

There was nothing to be gained by telling Kyle or the police, and everything to lose. So she would go home, carry on with life, and hope for the best.

As she sat beside Kyle on the bench, part of her realised the plan was an unviable one that had been made in a hungover upset haze. It wasn't sensible, clever or moral, and the talkers in her head were arguing about it full swing:

Tell him!

Don't tell him!

Just tell him.

Don't.

I killed Sarah!

Shut up.

But I killed her!

She was about to blurt it out when the bus arrived. Just in time.

Krissie sat alone and pressed her nose against the glass, squinting back towards the Devil's Staircase, an insignificant wriggle on an insignificant hill. She thought she could see something — a speck of purple maybe? The purple fabric of a tent, leaking out of a crack in the side of the hill? A hand in amongst the purple, grabbing at life, pleading to be found and not left there, please?

'Tickets!'

Krissie yelped so suddenly that the ticket inspector lost his balance.

'Sorry!' he said, righting himself with a grimace then marvelling at the state of the ticket bearer. Her eyes were red, she had bruises on her face and her hair was scraggly with a gash showing through.

Krissie handed over her ticket and looked back towards the hill. There was nothing there.

The bus passed through the bleakness of Crianlarich, towards the loch, then alongside farms and distilleries. The path that had taken so long to walk whizzed by her in a blur and suddenly she was surrounded by the houses of her city. Glasgow. It embraced her, the wetness and darkness of it, and she felt safer. She would disappear into it and be okay.

As the bus edged its way to Buchanan Street, Krissie turned her mobile on. She would ring her mum and dad and tell them she had blisters or such like, and had had a bit of a fall and then take Robbie home. Somehow she felt that being around her son would protect her. She could redeem herself as a mother, cocoon herself in the warmth of Robbie's need and forget everything. After all, it would be selfish to endanger Robbie's welfare by remembering.

Krissie waited for the bus to find its place, and disembarked. When her mobile rang, she stopped still in the middle of the terminal, terrified by it. Could it be the police? While hundreds of people stood huddled together looking up at a flickering electronic timetable, Krissie slowly, carefully, retrieved her phone from her jeans pocket.

The screen was blurred. She felt dizzy as she looked at it, unable to make out the words of the caller, but as the ringing seemed to get louder and louder, she thought she saw 'Sarah Mobile' written on the screen.

Krissie fell onto a bench as the next bus from Stirling was announced by an English accent to be arriving at 1443.

She gulped, pressed call back and listened for the ring.

But it didn't come.

What came instead was the bus from Stirling, at 1443, as predicted, and a low-battery warning signal and then nothing.

'I'm going crazy!' she thought to herself. 'I'm seeing things.'

In the taxi on the way to her parents' house Krissie kept thinking strange, dissonant thoughts like: one thing was for sure, a naturally guilt-ridden woman who is postnatally depressed should not have an affair with her best friend's husband and then murder the best friend. It doesn't help. In fact, it makes things significantly worse. If it hadn't been for the affair/murder episode, Krissie would have been well on the road to recovery.

As it stood, she was now in a haze of guilt-grief, unsure which to consider first. She had killed her best friend. She was a murderer and she would go to hell. Krissie hadn't believed in hell for some time, but now she did, and she would spend eternity in it.

Krissie considered the moment when everything changed, when she became the devil's daughter. It happened when Sarah said something about her being a liar and Krissie pushed her.

That split-second push had changed her from a normal everyday human being with reasonable flaws like drinking too much and being slightly vain and very impatient into a murderer. A split-second push, and things had changed forever.

She thought to herself that maybe that was why falling in love felt like grief, because with both, an identifiable single moment turns things upside down. You're cruising along quite easily and suddenly (with a kiss, or with a push), you take a sharp turn to the left or right, down towards hell.

As the taxi drove through Glasgow everything reminded Krissie of Sarah. She saw Sarah's face in every shop window, at every bus stop, at the church hall where they were Brownies together, at the park where they'd seesawed, at the chip shop where they'd smothered chips with curry sauce, at the hospital where Sarah had worked, at the street where Sarah grew up. Sarah. The friend she thought she would always have, always love. The friend she had killed.

23

When the taxi dropped me at the door of Mum and Dad's house, the haven where I had grown up, and Mum said, 'Kriss, darling, what's wrong? What are you doing home?' I nearly blurted, 'I came home, Mum, 'cause I killed Sarah!' Luckily I didn't. Luckily I said, 'I got blisters and had a bit of a fall and we fell out! Where's Robbie?' I asked.

Mum looked at me strangely, like everyone had been doing that day, and then asked me to quieten down.

'Robbie's asleep . . . ' she said, 'at last. Krissie, don't be alarmed, but he's under the weather.'

Mum had taken Robbie to hospital the night before after a long evening of unsettled crying. He'd been diagnosed with an ear infection and prescribed paracetamol and antibiotics. He'd be fine, as long as we kept his temperature down and as long as he completed the course of antibiotics. I rushed up to my old bedroom at the top of the stairs. Robbie was puffing away in the cot in the middle, his mouth open and his face red. I touched his burning cheek then raced back downstairs.

'How could you not have rung and told me?' I yelled at Mum. 'I'm his mother, for God's sake! I would have come back.'

'Shhh, Krissie, you'll wake him, love!' Dad said, shutting the door to the living room.

'We tried to call you, darlin' . . . You didn't answer.'

I hadn't had a tantrum for a long time. I hadn't stamped my feet, clenched my fists, and screamed. I let loose on this occasion with childish accusations about how they didn't trust me, how they didn't think I deserved him.

Then I gathered medicines and clothing and when Robbie (inevitably) woke up I rang a taxi.

Projection it's called. While I was guilty of adultery and murder, my parents were guilty of not summoning me back early enough to avoid adultery and murder. Better to concentrate on their guilt rather than mine, my subconscious had decided, much better.

While I waited for the taxi, Mum and Dad stared at me with worried looks on their faces.

'Stay here,' Dad said.

I didn't answer.

'You're in no state, darling,' Mum said.

I didn't answer.

'Or could I come with you?' Dad suggested.

'This is ridiculous, Krissie. You're being completely unreasonable.' My mum was getting angry. It was lucky that the taxi arrived before her anger broke my juvenile silence.

As the taxi joined the Clydeside Expressway I noticed that a police car — which was several vehicles behind us — joined too. It drove at forty miles an hour off the bridge and down the slip road, and then seemed to follow us along the Clyde, past the Tall Ship and the Exhibition Centre and the burnt-out antiques warehouse. We passed through three roundabouts and the cars between the police and us exited.

Was I being followed?

My heart raced as we drove down Dumbarton Road then up the steep tenement-lined Gardner Street. I peeked out the back window and saw that the police car had stopped on Dumbarton Road, where it waited.

I paid as fast as I could and stood with Robbie at the foot of my tenement building. The red sandstone hovered over me. I did not want to go up there, but as the taxi drove off I saw to my horror that the police car was coming up the hill.

I quickly opened the door to the close,

169

struggled upwards with my very heavy and now screaming child, went inside and locked the door.

I expected my flat to somehow reflect my state of mind but it was just as I'd left it: clean fresh wooden floors, artwork on the walls, lived-in eat in kitchen with loads of spices, comfortable sofas and floods of light. Back when I was happy, when I opened the door to my haven I would exhale with satisfaction and contentment. I would open the windows and let the air in.

This time, I cuddled Robbie then placed him under his baby gym, my gear beside the buggy in the hall, and raced around the house shutting all the blinds. Then I grabbed a bottle of red wine, opened it, and started drinking. From the living room, I had a good view of my street and the main road perpendicular to it. I peered through a crack in the wooden venetians and saw him there.

The cop.

Five-ten or so, hat on, radio and male. He was standing next to the cafe on the main road, obviously trying not to arouse suspicion.

It didn't work. I knew he was watching me. Knew that at any moment he would glance upwards inconspicuously to check that I was still in. Knew that he was waiting for armed cover to help raid my house, cuff my hands, drag me down the close, down the street, while my sick child looked on, the trauma staining his brain like beetroot.

He glanced up at the window, just as I suspected, and I quickly moved back from the blind.

I had to revise my plan.

I figured Matt must have found Sarah. Maybe I'd dropped something at the top of the cliff, or maybe there were marks from where Sarah fell. Somehow, he must have found her body and informed the police immediately.

In which case, I could either: come clean, lose Robbie and go to jail forever; or not come clean, not lose Robbie and not go to jail forever.

I decided on the second option, which meant I was on the run from the law.

I had never been on the run from the law before and my lack of experience made for poor and haphazard preparations.

First I booked two tickets to India over the internet. I would take Robbie to Goa, as I had such happy memories of my time there with Chas. We would live in a house, near a beach, out of reach. The tickets cost twelve hundred pounds altogether, which I put on Visa.

Next I took my phone and intercom off the hook and turned off the computer.

Then I packed passports. Luckily Robbie had one after the whole Italy trip disaster. At least something positive had come out of it — we could not only run from the law, we could fly from it.

Next I shoved some clothes, toiletries and headache tablets into my rucksack.

After that I wrote a letter to Mum and Dad and then ripped it up and wrote another one and then ripped that up. What could I tell them?

I peered through the crack in the venetians again and saw the cop still standing there. I wouldn't be able to leave via the front door. I looked out the back. Marco was doing something in the communal bin area. I would have to escape from the flat another way.

I remembered the old bag's flat opposite mine had been broken into via the loft once. The guy had crawled in through the small square opening in the shared close and bashed through the ceiling of the bathroom.

I decided I would do the same — crawl through the lofts of these interconnected tenements, exit through another manhole in another close and walk out. Simple.

Robbie had calmed down. The Calpol Mum had given him had kicked in, and he was wriggling happily on the padded blanket of his baby gym, banging his fists against ducks and squeaky balls and smiling. I left him in the living room and went to check the route.

I opened my front door and made sure there was no-one around, then dislodged the wooden door from the manhole and pulled myself up and into the loft. It was a dusty wooden place filled with insulation, random pieces of plywood and an artificial Christmas tree. I crawled along the beams, past specks of light, but very quickly reached a dead end. It was bricked up. I crawled the other way, estimating the size of my flat and the size of the one opposite me, and realised that the lofts were not interconnected at all; they were separated by the gradient of the hill and by bricks.

When I jumped back down to the close, dust and insulation followed me. Alerted by the noise, the old bag across the landing peered at me through the glass of her front door. I ran inside and shut the door.

There was no way of escaping through the roof. I would have to sneak out the back.

Robbie was still playing on his mat and had rolled onto his tummy. He held his head up with excitement and kicked his legs on the ground.

I dressed myself in celebrity disguise — coat, glasses, hat, scarf — then put my rucksack on my back, picked up Robbie and hid him under my coat. He thought this was tremendous fun, and began eating the straps of my rucksack with wet, determined gums.

I walked down the close and made my way to the back door, but Marco was coming in from the bins.

'Krissie? What are you doing?' he asked.

'Just heading out for a walk.'

I turned around and walked towards the front door. It would look altogether too weird to go out the back.

When I opened the door to the outside world I saw the policeman. He was sitting at an outside table drinking a coffee. I upped the pace and headed in the opposite direction.

Walk fast, my talkers said, don't stop, don't look, get down Gardner Street to the taxi rank on Dumbarton Road, just walk fast, don't stop.

'Krissie!'

I ignored the voice and walked fast, not stopping.

'Krissie Donald!'

I ran down the hill. But so did the cop. And he was fast. He was gaining on me.

'Krissie!'

His arm grabbed mine and I had no choice. I had to stop. The tears were ready to flow, the penance was ready to be said. I turned to face up.

'Don't tell me you don't recognise me?'

'Sorry?' I said, surprised that a policeman nabbing a murderess would speak in this familiar, relaxed, almost excited tone.

'It's Johnny, Constable Johnny Wallace!'

With this statement, I realised that I was not in trouble, that I was safe and did not have to run off to India never to be seen again. Unfortunately, though, I had no idea who Johnny Wallace was.

'Oh, hi!' I said, turning my head to the side a little to see if he looked familiar from a different angle.

'You really don't recognise me?'

I said I was sorry as adorably as I could and he leant towards me and whispered in my ear. 'Clatty Patty's? Then yours?'

'Ah,' I said, still tilting my head to the side and squinting.

Annoyed by my obvious lack of recognition, his tone changed. Hitherto his voice had oozed, 'Hey, look at me, I'm a cop!' Henceforth it would ooze, 'You'd better watch your step, girly-girl!'

With this tone in place he stepped back and said: 'We had sex twice and in the morning you called me a taxi because I didn't know the first line of *Anna Karenina*.'

I remembered him! The sex had been good but he was two coupons short of a toaster. 'That was a penultimate experience!' he'd said jubilantly after coming.

'Oh,' I said. 'I'm so sorry! Of course. You look great! Lovely to see you. I'd better get going, though.'

He raised his eyebrows and toyed with his truncheon threateningly as I said goodbye and headed back towards my flat.

'Ms Donald!' he yelled after me.

I froze and a girly-girl voice came at me from behind.

'*Happy families are all alike; every unhappy family is unhappy in its own way . . .* '

I turned around, attempted to smile at him, and then walked back to my flat.

Once inside, I put Robbie back under his baby gym and he immediately rolled over onto his front. This was new, this vigorous rolling, and he seemed very pleased with himself about it. After nine months of doing very little, of lying around like a blob, I thought fleetingly, it must seem quite exciting to roll over.

I went to the bathroom to wash my face. In the mirror was a woman with red eyes, bruises, bag-lady hair and very odd clothes. Who was I? And what was I thinking? Hoping for the best? Escaping? I couldn't get away from this, away from my guilt, ever. I had to tell.

I was about to ring the police when I heard an enormous bang from the kitchen. I ran into the dark room and looked around. Nothing was out of place. As I turned to leave the kitchen I heard another loud bang. It was the window. The window had banged. I walked towards it slowly, and gently nudged one of the venetian slats upwards. Putting my eye against the slit, I looked out towards the evening sky and then down towards the drying green below, where I saw Sarah standing, dressed in a shapeless purple tent, her white dislocated arm trailing behind her.

I dropped the slat and ran to the front door to check the lock. It was secure. I put the chain on and then raced around the bedrooms checking the windows. They were all shut, but the banging started again.

Bang. Bang. Bang. The thud echoed in my head, from the front door this time. *Bang. Bang. Bang.*

It was Shakespearean. Sarah was obviously trying to get in. Her ghost was coming to get me.

I raced into the living room to get Robbie

and stopped dead over the little padded mattress of the baby gym that he'd been lying on seconds earlier.

He wasn't there.

She'd taken him! Sarah's ghost had taken my son!

'Robbie! Robbie, where are you? ROBBIE!' I shrieked, terrified.

I raced around the flat. Into the bathroom, behind the shower curtain. In the kitchen, under the table, in the pantry. Then I ran into the bedroom, sobbing hysterically as the banging continued on the front door. I searched frantically in the wardrobe and behind the curtains and under the bed.

And there he was. Eating fluff from under my king-size bed. I looked at him and he smiled, with fluff on his bottom lip, and then all of a sudden he crawled towards me on all fours with a huge grin.

My baby was crawling!

I gathered him in my arms and moved back into the hall. The banging had stopped.

When I looked out the kitchen window again I saw a large Apple Mac box in the rubbish area with some ripped bubble wrap floating in the wind behind it.

I was seeing things. I was mad.

I walked from the kitchen to the hall and the banging started again, moving up a gear.

To my horror, the front door began to move and shake.

I tucked Robbie under my lilac fleece as the door throbbed and shook. Stepping back towards the wall of the living room, I slid downwards to the floor, resigned, with Robbie in my arms. We were huddled together in a ball of whimpering purple, waiting.

We watched as the bottom hinge splintered from the wall, as the chain brace screw loosened and plopped to the floor, as the top hinge broke off suddenly and as the brace of the mortice lock fractured from the wall.

The door fell onto the floor before us, as if in slow motion, with a whoosh and a thud and a gust of air.

When I looked up, the door was flat before me, and a pair of legs were behind it. I followed the denim-clad legs, which I was sure were the legs of the ghost of Sarah, slowly upwards . . . towards the stomach I was sure was the stomach of dead Sarah . . . towards a face that under no circumstances was the face of Sarah.

Because it was the face of Chas.

24

After leaving Krissie's parents, Chas had gone home to a fantastic welcome from his family in Edinburgh. Unable to get Krissie out of his mind he tried to get hold of her on her mobile. She wasn't answering, so he phoned Krissie's mum to check he had the right number. Anna told him the holiday had been a disaster. They'd argued. She'd had a fall. And Krissie had come home. Chas could tell from Anna's voice that she was really upset.

'I just don't know what to do anymore,' she told Chas. 'We don't seem to be getting through to her at all. Dave's trying to persuade me that we need to get away. I have to admit, we're both pretty exhausted. He's found some internet deal or other.'

'You should,' Chas said.

'But I need to check on her.'

'I'll check on her,' Chas said. 'You head off and get some rest.'

'Are you sure?' Anna said. 'Maybe that would be a good idea ... Maybe she'd respond better to you ... But ring us. Let us know how you get on.'

During the fifty-minute train journey back to Glasgow, Chas thought about Krissie. He'd been in love with her for years. Since he'd first clapped eyes on her eating curry with her hands in a beach cafe in Goa, trying hard to be cool and local but doing it all wrong. Their eyes had locked. Hers were bright blue and deep, and they shone with energy and inquisitiveness.

After he got to know her he loved her feistiness, her determination, her body, her looks, her brain, her jeans, the books she read, the job she wanted to do, everything.

But somehow she'd remained oblivious to his feelings for her, and consistently went for arseholes, guys who pretended to like her independence and feminism, then changed their minds when their chemicals merged. Chas hadn't wanted to blow his chances, so he'd waited and waited, and they became the best of mates. There was that one time, when he'd kissed her in a taxi, when he'd wanted to fly to the moon with the thrill of it, but all she'd said was 'yuck'.

* * *

As Chas walked towards Krissie's flat he could tell someone was in — lights had gone on and then off, blinds had gone up and then down — but Krissie didn't answer her intercom, her landline or her mobile.

Chas rang her buzzer, but she didn't answer. Then he tossed several stones at the kitchen window. He then rang all the buzzers in the close. Eventually, a young guy let him in.

When he got to the top floor, the old lady from across the way was watching through the window of her front door. Chas gave her a half-smile then knocked on Krissie's door several times. He could hear strange noises coming from inside the flat, but no-one came to the door.

'Be careful,' the neighbour said, coming out of her flat to join him. 'It could be a burglar. I was broken into a while back, you know. They took the diamond brooch my great-grandmother from Portree gave my grandmother . . . Should I ring the police?'

'No, just give me a sec,' Chas said, wary of police involvement so soon after his release.

Chas put his ear against the door. He could hear her in there, rushing around and yelling for her son, and he panicked and kicked the door in as the old lady watched with horror. This wasn't a two or three kick affair; it took him ages and he seriously hurt his right foot and lower back in the process.

When the door came down, he saw Krissie sitting there, huddled and quivering with her little boy in her arms. It took her a few moments to recognise him, but when she did she breathed out hard and began to sob.

Chas held them both in his arms. His darling Krissie and her beautiful little bundle of a boy.

'Sarah! She's in purple!' she muttered, over and over again.

She was delirious, not making sense. He took her into the bedroom and laid her down.

Chas told the neighbour there was no burglar and no need to call the police. Then he placed the door upright and fed Robbie who eventually fell asleep. Chas returned to Krissie's bedroom, where she was lying with her eyes closed. It was dark outside now and Chas turned off the bedside light so Krissie could sleep.

'Sarah!' she said again.

'You're not well, baby girl, you're not making sense. Get some sleep!'

Then she opened her eyes and said, 'Chas, how did it feel, doing something really bad?'

'I didn't do anything really bad.'

'How can you say that?'

'Never you mind, off you go to sleep.'

Krissie drifted off into a restless sleep, visions of Sarah's face haunting her dreams.

Blood and death with a sickly smile.

'Krissie! Kriss! Clever clogs,' said Sarah through her bloody mouth.

Krissie woke with a jolt and then drifted off again, mumbling in her sleep. 'I slept with Kyle! I'm so sorry, Sarah. Kyle!'

As Chas watched Krissie tossing and turning in bed, he realised she was in a terrible mess. She looked ragged and drawn — and from what she was saying, it seemed pretty obvious she had committed adultery with Kyle. If she continued on this path, Chas thought to himself, she would spiral downwards and downwards. If only she could see that with him to love her and take care of her . . .

As her conscious world finally came into view again Krissie sprang up and crushed Chas's hopes with her words: 'Can you look after Robbie for a while? I have to go and see Kyle.'

She dressed quickly, as if in a panic, and raced off into the darkness.

After she left, Chas sat beside Robbie and looked at his little face. His bottom lip was tucked in under his top one, his hands were curled under his chin and his eyelashes seemed so long and dark that it was hard not to believe he had mascara on. He was so like his mum.

Chas was thinking about the time Krissie tickled him on the floor and he told her she was the most beautiful woman in the universe, when an alarm rang outside, jolting him back into the present.

Prison had imbued Chas with a fear of alarms. It started in the middle of his sentence. An alarm rang after lights out one night and kept on ringing. He was on the top bunk and had no cell mate at the time. He lay there on his back as he heard officers yell and keys jingle and then slowly got off his bunk, stepped down onto the concrete floor, and looked out of his tiny square peephole. The door to the cell opposite him was open, and a man was hanging from the top bunk, his jeans tight around his neck, his knees dragging on the floor, and his head bright purple. The dead man swung around towards the peephole and his bulging eyes looked straight into Chas's. An officer was vomiting into the sink down the hall and someone was dialling a code blue, code blue.

When Chas returned to his bunk, the purple dead man seemed to have moved in below him, never to be liberated.

So when Chas heard this alarm, he jumped up, his head pounding. He moved the front door out of the way and walked onto the landing, and then down to the bottom of the stairs. The alarm got louder and louder as Chas looked out the front door onto the street and then opened the front door.

He stepped out onto the street and saw that the alarm was coming from a car. He looked at the car for some time. Would it just keep going? Would no-one do anything? How do things work out here?

Then the front door shut.

He grabbed hold of the handle and tried to open it.

Locked.

'Shit!'

Too embarrassed to ring the buzzers again, Chas ran around to the back of the flats and climbed over the brick wall of the communal gardens. A sensor light went on and made it hard for him to see the back door, but he found it eventually and turned the handle.

The alarm was so loud that it almost blew him off his feet, and lights in the eight flats above him came on one by one. He yelled at the faces in the windows: 'Let me in . . . The baby's upstairs!' To his relief, the dopey young man who'd let him in earlier opened his window.

'What?' asked Marco.

'Let me in. There's a baby alone in the flat above you.'

'In Krissie's flat?'

'Aye, aye. Let me in.'

Marco thought for a moment, shut the window and called the police.

25

I got out of the taxi, approached the door, knocked, and stood in the darkness for a moment. As the rowan tree snowed brown and yellow leaves in the breeze, I thought I heard a whisper.

'Krissie! Krissie!'

I turned around and looked at the leaves falling to the ground and then I saw Sarah — her white and red body — flesh and blood.

'Krissie! KRISSIE!'

Kyle's voice made me jump and I turned with a gasp.

There were several half-packed suitcases in the hall.

'Krissie!'

I looked back at the tree — Sarah wasn't there, just a tree trunk.

'I need to talk to you,' I whispered.

He let me in and we walked awkwardly to the kitchen.

Kyle said he hadn't seen Sarah, that she was probably still at the cottage on Loch Katrine and wasn't answering his calls. He was going to stay at his folks for a bit so she could come home in peace if she wanted and —

'She's not at Loch Katrine,' I interrupted.

'Have you spoken to her?'

'No.'

'What do you mean then?'

I blurted it out as fast as I could to get it over with, how she'd followed me that night, how we'd argued and she'd attacked me, how I'd pushed her, she'd fallen, I'd found her dead and hid her . . .

He swayed on his feet and then his eyes filled heavily with tears. He took his hand away from his mouth, breathing hard and oddly. Then his face distorted in grief and he made a ferocious groan and fell to his knees.

I tried to touch him, bent down to hold him, but he flicked me off and changed demeanour again.

'You murdering bitch!'

He got up and began pounding on my chest. I took it, all the while saying, 'It was an accident and I panicked. I didn't mean it!'

He stopped hitting me and buried himself in me, sobbing uncontrollably into my chest.

'I'm so sorry, so sorry . . . ' I cried.

Over his shoulders, my eyes zoomed in on the island unit, where the silver phone sat, waiting.

I gathered his face in my hands and looked into his eyes.

'I'm going to call the police now,' I said.

He was splotchy and drenched and he stared at me before a flicker of his professional calm returned: 'NO! Krissie, no! You can't call the police.'

He decided we should not tell anyone. Because of our affair, he would be a suspect and lose everything and I would lose Robbie. Instead, he would drive to Glencoe with the necessary equipment, and dispose of Sarah's body properly. He would leave now and get it done by dawn, when he would text me. Under no circumstances should I contact him and we should never see each other again.

I argued with him. It was no use running away from this, I said. It would always be there, haunting us. But he insisted, rather angrily. 'We will both go to jail. They saw us dancing in the hotel, heard you two arguing in the foyer, everyone must have known we had an affair for God's sake! What will it look like? We'll both get life!'

He started rushing around the house gathering things, asking me to describe exactly where the crevice was, rummaging under the sink for black bin liners . . .

'Don't contact me,' he insisted, leading me to the back door. 'I'll text you when it's done. I'll text *yes*, that's all, just *yes* and you'll know. Now go.' He ignored my protests and pushed me through the door.

'Go out by the lane and don't let anyone see you!' Then he slammed the door behind me.

I ran to the gate and into the dark lane where I stumbled into a brown wheelie bin. An enormous bang went off nearby, terrifying me until I realised it was local kids setting off fireworks. Guy Fawkes is coming, I thought to myself, before running for three miles as if Sarah's sickly ghost was at my heels.

It was about ten at night when I reached my tenement. Most of the buildings in the area were turning lights off for the night, but mine seemed to have every single light on. Each of the eight flats, two on each level, were bright with life. I entered the close and heard lots of voices. They got louder and louder and several doors were open on the way up.

The old bag opposite was peering through her glass again and my door was no longer propped up precariously against the wall, but lying on the floor. I stepped over it and could hear several people talking in the living room. I checked Robbie's room to make sure he was okay — he was sleeping soundly in his cot — and then walked into the living room.

There, on the two comfy sofas, were Chas, Constable Johnny Wallace, and the too-pretty policewoman who had appeared at my door the week before the holiday, plus a twin-set and pearls social worker and her pale gay apprentice.

'What's going on?' I asked.

They were very polite, now that I look back, but I didn't take it well. They'd been called by Marco after Chas got locked out with Robbie inside. They'd interviewed neighbours who'd heard banging and shouting in the evening, heard me crawling around in the loft, seen me dressed oddly and trying to run away down Gardner Street, then heard a man shouting up that there was a baby alone in the flat. And this wasn't the first time I'd left the child alone, as the young policewoman pointed out. There'd been an incident about a week earlier.

'I told you I was doing controlled crying!' I argued pathetically. 'And anyway, this time Chas was looking after him!'

'Mr Worthington left the building,' said the female cop.

'I popped out when I heard an alarm, and the door slammed on me!' Chas argued.

I could have killed him.

'Do you realise Mr Worthington has just been released from prison and is currently on parole?' This from Pearls, the social worker.

'Yes, I do. Okay!' I said, and sat down to try and be sensible. 'I'm a social worker myself, a child protection social worker. I've worked in the Gorbals office for years, so I understand completely why you're here. I've got loads of children on supervision who really *are* in danger, whose parents really aren't able to look after them. But this isn't the same. I know what I'm doing. I'm from a good family! I've had a very difficult couple of days, and I'm very sorry, but I'm back now, and Robbie's fine, so if it's okay, I'll just see you out . . . '

26

As a social worker, I had been on the other side many times. I'd argued against teenagers whose parents couldn't control them and I'd reported on their progress in assessment centres or secure units. I'd written about mothers who were not trying hard enough to break their heroin habits and told fathers that they could not have any contact with their children because this time they had gone too far.

Now here I was, on the other side. The really awful side. The side where the poor people of Glasgow usually sit, with middle-class arseholes — like me — on the other side making decisions about their lives and their children's based on the books they'd read, on the information they'd gathered, on the visits they'd made, and on their interpretations of the things you'd said to them.

'I'm afraid it's not as simple as that,' said Pearls haughtily.

I sighed, realising I was in deep shit. My fitness as a mother was being judged by this lot. And as they put their concerns to me, the ground I was standing on became increasingly flimsy by the second.

I'd left Robbie alone before and my repetition of the controlled crying argument in relation to that was not washing.

I'd taken stress leave, Pearls discovered after making a few calls, so my argument about being a capable social worker did not wash.

I smelt of drink and there were a dozen empty wine bottles in the kitchen. My argument about a forthcoming expedition to the recycling bin was not washing.

All but Pearls had working-class accents, so my argument about being from a 'good family' must have been a particularly irritating one.

I clearly had rather questionable acquaintances, Pearls implied, looking pointedly at Chas, and my argument about Chas being a good guy despite his criminal record and recent child neglect did not wash.

I had wild eyes, bruises, a gash on my head and my argument about just needing some sleep was not washing.

My parents were not answering any of their phones, and I had no other relatives in Glasgow, so my argument about my family always being on call did not wash.

And the policewoman's suggestion that I

contact my friend Sarah from the previous incident and have her stay for the night did not wash either because I had 'no idea where she is, honestly! No idea at all! We've been away camping but how should I know where she is now?'

'But if we can contact her, would you be happy for Sarah to take him, until you feel better?' she asked.

'Yes, of course,' I said.

I gave them several phone numbers and they made several calls, then I barricaded Robbie's bedroom as Pale Gay and Pearls moved towards it.

Just for the night, they said, you need some rest, just till you calm down. There's nothing to worry about.

I blocked them with my arms as they tried to enter.

We'll try ringing your mum and Sarah, they said, we'll keep trying, but he'll be fine for the night, in a safe place.

I stood in front of the cot as they tried to get at him.

We'll organise an emergency hearing tomorrow, they soothed, we'll work something out then.

I clutched at Robbie as they prised him from me.

It's just for the night, they said, just till you

sober up and get some support.

I cried with mouth wide open as they walked through the hall.

We'll keep ringing your friend, they said, and your mum.

As they walked over the flattened door I screamed, 'He's got an ear infection! You need his medicine! Keep his temperature down or he'll be in terrible pain!'

Pearls took the Boots bag from me and walked down the steps with my beautiful baby boy in her arms.

I sat on the floor of my messy weirdo flat, smelling of alcohol and sweat, eyes red raw, hysteria oozing from me, and said to myself, 'Of course they had to take him. They had no choice . . . I'd have done the same!'

I then looked up and saw Chas standing there sheepishly.

'You have to go,' I said.

He didn't move.

'Get out!' I yelled. 'GET OUT!'

My yell convinced him to withdraw. He walked from the hall, placed the broken door back up in its precarious position, and left me there with my ruined empty arsehole life.

* * *

It was probably several hours before I scraped myself from the floor of the hall and walked to the living room. I looked blankly at the photos on my mantelpiece — Sarah and Kyle at the university chapel; my parents smiling as they hiked in the Pyrenees; Robbie in the cot at the Queen Mother's Hospital. Things that had been certain in my life, things that were no longer.

What should I go crazy about first?

Killing Sarah?

Losing Robbie?

Chas?

Kyle? He was driving north with a saw and knives and several large refuse sacks in his boot. He would text me with yes to say that it was done rather than ever lay eyes on me again, so — for now — all I could do was wait for the beep-beep.

And then I remembered I had not recharged my phone. I plugged it in and waited for it to come to life, and when it did I saw that there was only one missed call, not from the police, not from Kyle, but from Mum and Dad.

I looked at the clock. It was six am. Kyle would be finished by now. He would have chopped Sarah's body into pieces and put them in the innocent black bags.

Jesus, this had to stop. It had to stop. I

phoned him but he didn't answer. I tried and tried. 'This mobile is switched off,' a recorded voice kept droning. 'Please leave a . . . '

I made a decision. With or without Kyle's approval, I would have a shower, get dressed, and ready myself for a confession at Drumgoyne Police Station. Robbie would be better off with my parents.

I took a last look around my living room. Everywhere in the room were hints of a happy life — the baby gym, ornaments from holidays in Spain and Italy, a photo of Mum and Dad getting married, the photo of my christening, Chas, Kyle and I at university, Sarah and I at her wedding, me and Robbie on the swing in Mum and Dad's garden. As I looked around at these relics of happiness, I realised that I had been given the most perfect life that any person could have.

So as I sat there looking at the ornaments and thinking about my wonderful life, what I wanted to know was this: how had I managed to screw it up so badly?

27

Chas could have told Krissie the answer to her question. He knew.

He was sitting on the step outside the front door of Krissie's tenement, waiting for her to calm down, revising his apology and his plan. He could not believe he'd caused so much harm in so little time, and he hated himself for it, because he of all people knew that what Krissie needed was nurturing, not hassle.

After Chas decided to quit medicine, his parents blew a gasket. His sister, by then an advocate in Edinburgh, came and tried to talk him out of it, but he wouldn't listen. Could they not see that this was the right thing for him to do? He told them he wanted to see the world. He wanted to do something creative. Write or paint? He wasn't sure yet. All he knew was that he didn't want to be a doctor. He didn't want to have loads of money. He didn't want to have a golf club membership or an investment property or a Mercedes. He needed to see things and feel things and be everything that he could possibly be, and then maybe come home — but not before he had really experienced himself.

Kyle was even worse than his family. 'What a waste! What a quitter,' he'd said.

But Krissie's mum, Anna, had been just what the non-doctor ordered. She showed up with a bottle of wine and several packets of crisps and set up bar in the bay window.

'You know, Chas, sometimes people are just plain scared of what other people's reactions will be. If you do what everyone says you should do, you'll wake up one day and you'll be dead.'

They talked for hours that night. Kyle was on holidays at the time, and Krissie was going out with some thug from Aberdeen, so the place was all theirs. Anna told him how she'd done mad things before she settled down and she was so damn glad she had, because now she had nothing to regret and nothing to prove. She liked everything about her life and about herself except perhaps her leathery neck.

Chas talked to Anna about painting, how he felt happy when he had a brush in his hand. Since leaving medicine he'd been working three jobs to save for travelling, and had spent every spare minute painting in his room.

When the conversation moved to relation-ships, Chas said, 'You and Dave are so happy,

so at ease. If you don't mind me asking . . . '
Chas hesitated.

'You're going to ask me why Krissie isn't
that way.'

She was right, that was exactly what he was
going to ask her. Krissie was full of life,
brimming with it. When she walked into the
room, she was luminous. She was lubrication
for an awkward party, tonic for a depressed
friend in need. But when it came to
relationships, she was a disaster.

Anna looked at him very seriously. 'You're
in love with her, aren't you, Chas?'

After a pause Anna told Chas a story that
would shape the next ten years of his life, and
which had been shaping Krissie's since she
was six.

Chas was enraged by what Anna told him.
Everything suddenly fell into place.

'Don't do anything stupid!' Anna told him.
'For Krissie's sake.'

He promised her he wouldn't, repeated
after her that there would be nothing to gain
from taking matters into his own hands.

'She just needs time,' Anna said. 'Just give
her some time.'

The next day, Chas left Glasgow for his
second big trip. He worked in bars and
sketched in the Himalayas and met the Dalai
Lama and rode on a camel through Rajasthan

and painted in Malaysia and Thailand, wrote in Vietnam and painted in Bali and then at Uluru.

In every sketch or painting he did, she was there — behind a door, on a rock, swimming in the sea — always there, the woman he was giving time.

Then he came home. A painter. Unafraid of the world, knowing what he was and what he wanted to do, and wanting to share it all with the woman he adored.

28

Kyle left Glasgow around 11 p.m. He had all the equipment he needed in his emergency medical bag, and drove flat out to Glencoe in under three hours. His plan was to steal one of the luggage trolleys from the hotel, wheel Sarah's chopped body back to his car, and dump it in the quarry they'd walked past near Inverarnan.

When Kyle got to the hotel the door was open and no-one was in the foyer. He tiptoed in and glanced around, but the luggage trolleys were nowhere to be seen. He searched for one in the steel kitchen area, then ran up the stairs to the first floor, where he found one sitting beside the lift. After jerking it down the stairs and through the foyer, he started along the path.

The luggage trolley was a bad idea. Kyle had never walked a baby in a buggy or a disabled person in a wheelchair along cobblestones. If he had, he'd have known that wheels and bumpy paths do not mix. The trolley jarred and twisted at every turn, and after fifty metres he ditched it. It might take two trips, but it was only 2.13 am so he had plenty of time. He left the trolley at the side of the mountain and walked on, his torch tickling the path with balls of weak light.

Kyle followed Krissie's instructions, abandoning the track about halfway up, then scrambling to the top of the cliff, stopping when he could go no further.

He saw the ridge to the right and climbed down, just as Krissie had done, quickly spotting the first cave she described. Following her instructions, he strode another thirty metres and began to search for the crevice.

An hour later he was still frantically scrabbling about. It was 4.25 a.m., and he was running out of time. He would have to lug Sarah's body in one trip.

A surge of fear sped through him when he heard a loud scratching noise. Must have been a bird, he reassured himself, looking around and seeing no-one else. The scratching continued and he couldn't see a bird — or any animal — anywhere near him, so he followed the scratching noise along the ground until it got so loud he thought it must have been coming from under his feet. He knelt down and scraped some dirt away, but the noise stopped. He shook his head. He was losing his mind. He sat up and rested his head against the cliff face, only to open his eyes again suddenly when the scratching resumed. He sat, eyes wide open, for a full three seconds, and then turned his head around slowly until his torch was pointing directly at the heather-covered, rock-filled crevice Krissie had described.

The scratching got louder as he stood up and pulled at the largest rock, which was lodged at the top of the opening. It fell with a thump to the ground.

Kyle stared into blackness for a moment; the sound was so loud now that it seemed to echo through the valley. His heartbeat was almost as loud as the scratching, and when the noise stopped, it felt like his heart did too. No breathing, no noise, nothing, only darkness and silence.

Just as Kyle was about to relax, a dark shape sprang at him from the crevice, catapulting his heart back into action.

'Jesus!' he yelled, then began to breathe more easily again as the rat scuttled off into the scrub. A fucking rat!

He turned around again and faced the black hole that was the rat's home. The darkness of it was terrifying and he trembled as he and his torch moved closer to have a look inside. Slowly, a centimetre at a time, he moved forward . . . almost there now, almost . . .

The hand fell out and hit his face. A white, thin, bony hand.

Kyle let out a scream of absolute unadulterated terror as he flicked the dead hand off. But after throwing the arm back towards the crevice, he realised that this hand was not dead.

This hand was alive.

Kyle pulled the rest of the rocks from the crevice with almost superhuman strength. As the last rock fell to the ground, the stench of the enclosure hit him and he gagged. Covering his mouth and nose, he peered into the crevice. His wife opened her eyes and looked back. She was pale and bloody and stinking. Her body and one arm were wrapped in the purple tent. The other arm was loose, and looked strangely disconnected.

'Sarah, it's okay. I've come to get you. It's all right,' he said as he pulled her out of the crevice, unravelling her as quickly as he could, and gagging once again as the smell of her hit the air.

He checked her breathing and her pulse, then sat her up and held her and cried.

'Oh, thank God, Sarah, you're alive. Sarah, my Sarah. Thank God. My darling.'

29

It had been a long, excruciatingly painful twenty-three hours for Sarah, but quite therapeutic in the end.

She had learnt a lot about herself and about her past and had made some very sensible plans for the future — if she had one.

She'd regained consciousness about two hours after Krissie had left her. It was completely dark and she had a very normal response to waking up injured, wrapped in a tent, covered in blood, shoved in a crevice and left to die. After the initial shock started to wear off, she cried, shook and tried to scream.

Sarah was surprised by how long she maintained her hysteria. Despite several hindrances — she couldn't move, couldn't see anything, and couldn't sustain a yell because her mouth was cut and swollen — she was still the champion of all panickers.

'I'm gonna die, I'm gonna die, I'm gonna die.' She said over and over again, for at least two hours.

She'd had a lot of practice, right enough. From the age of six she'd enjoyed regular panic attacks, usually triggered by being trapped in small spaces. She became aware of this at Marie Johnston's sixth birthday party when, while playing hide-and-seek, she ran into Marie's attic, and squeezed through a small door and into the dark eaves of the house. She giggled for a few seconds after closing the door before realising just how dark and dusty the place was, and then decided to get the hell out. Only she couldn't. Because Marie and her brother Willie were holding the door shut.

'Let me out!' she'd screamed.

But they didn't. They thought it was funny. And Sarah found herself experiencing something that a six-year-old should not experience. She honestly thought she was going to die.

Eventually Marie's mum came up to the attic to see what all the giggling was about and opened the door to find Sarah sweating profusely, rocking back and forth, and chanting, 'I'm gonna die, I'm gonna die, I'm gonna die.'

From then on, Sarah made sure to check every situation for escape routes. In movies, she sat in the aisle at the back. She never took the lift, never sat at the back of the bus, never used the underground, and spent the first few minutes anywhere new checking out the exits.

When they'd played 'face up' at the loch

a few nights earlier, Krissie and Kyle didn't realise that the sleeping bag was no problem for her. She had the zipper in her hand. To get out, all she had to do was pull at it. At no point during the fifteen minutes in that sleeping bag did she think she was going to die. There was an escape route.

This problem with enclosed spaces had come up in one of her therapy sessions. But the therapist didn't believe it started in Marie Johnston's attic, especially once Sarah had admitted to having had similar fears for a year prior to that. The therapist believed it started at home, and dedicated the following sessions to trying to tear the truth about her childhood out of her piece by piece.

But Sarah did not break.

Okay, so when she was tiny her mother was away all the time, but she rang every night at bedtime.

Okay, so her father drank a bit, but then he left.

Okay, so her parents split up when she was five, but Sarah loved her new stepdad. He was a movie producer who made the best hot chocolate with marshmallows and had given her a signed poster of Mel Gibson.

No big deal. A normal messed-up family

like everyone else had.

No big deal at all.

* * *

After the initial burst of anger and panic in the crevice, Sarah fell unconscious again.

When she woke again she wasn't sure if she'd opened her eyes or not, because no matter what she did with her eyelids, it was still dark. It took a few moments to realise the terrifying truth, and it was impossible not to revert to hysteria. She was wrapped so tightly that she couldn't move her hand, or her feet, or any other part of her body. It was so small, the space, that her nose touched the rock above her, the damp, cold rock. Her legs were bent sideways, so that her hips were in agony, and her shoulder was roaring with pain.

She was buried alive and she was going to die. Every organ switched on to high alert, adrenalin attacked each limb to DO SOME-THING. But she could not move, she could not do anything, and so the adrenalin buzzed around inside her trying to escape, like a bee in a jar.

She must have fainted over and over again, and every time she woke the bee, now a sworn enemy of hers, attacked her again. She became so aware of it that she could almost track its path around her, and could sense its slowing, from thousands of miles an hour to hundreds, to tens, to nothing.

To banish the noise, she spoke out loud through her swollen mouth and her voice scared her. It sounded like she had earphones on.

'I'm going to be okay,' she told herself. 'I'm going to be fine. I have to think logically.'

So she asked and answered as many questions as she could think of out loud, as if she was a doctor gathering information to diagnose a patient.

Can I move my legs?

No, they're tied or wrapped — in a tent, I think.

Can I wriggle my toes?

Yes, I can wriggle my toes.

Is there enough air?

There are three cracks at least in the rocks. Don't worry about that.

What the hell is that?

An arm.

I'm going to die. Oh my God.

You're going to be fine.

Whose arm?

Oh my God, it's my arm. What's it doing there? I'm fucked. I'm buried alive.

You're not fucked. Your arm is dislocated but it's okay. You will be okay.

She worked out that she was wrapped in a tent up to her neck. She knew she didn't have the use of arms or legs to help push out the rocks, even though they didn't seem to be very securely lodged in the crack, she knew that her throat was aching for water, and that she was absolutely dying for a shit.

To keep her mind off the latter, she decided to make a plan. Only a month before, she'd watched a documentary about a guy who'd been left for dead on a mountain in the Andes. He spent days crawling with a broken leg through ice and mountains, and eventually made it home. The way he did it was to take things one small step at a time.

If I can just get to that rock.

If I can just make it over that ledge.

If I can just slide down that fissure.

So that's how Sarah spent the next while. The first task was to free her left arm from the tent.

If I can just wriggle enough to loosen the tent from around my body.

If I can just wriggle my hip twice to the right.

If I can just wriggle my hip twice to the left.

So she wriggled.

And wriggled.

Again.

Then again.

And every now and then she fooled herself into believing that she had made progress, but eventually she had to admit that for each wriggle that loosened the tent, there was a wriggle that tightened it.

★ ★ ★

She had been in the dark silence for hours when her phone burst into noise. It was 'Scotland the Brave'.

Hark when the night is falling,
Hear! hear, the pipes are calling,
Loudly and proudly calling,
Down thro' the glen
There where the hills are sleeping,
Now feel the blood a-leaping,
High as the spirits
of the old Highland men.

Towering in gallant fame,
Scotland my mountain hame,
High may your proud
standards gloriously wave.
Land of my high endeavour,
Land of the shining river,
Land of my heart forever
Scotland the brave.

It was piercing, thin and interminable and it was coming from her jacket pocket.

After the initial fright, she tried to be logical again.

One of her arms was dislocated and behind her neck. She could not get to the answer button with this arm.

The other was wrapped so tightly within the rolled fabric of the tent that she would never dislodge it.

Her legs were in the recovery position, knees slightly bent, but after several attempts to bring her knees towards her chest she realised that it was not going to happen. The crevice was too small, her legs were too tightly encased, and her boobs were too fucking big.

She rested when it stopped, and cried. Her only hope gone with the shining river.

She had not been resting long when it started again.

Over the next few hours, the phone rang ten times. Sarah became well acquainted with the stages of grieving, and gave each her all as the song rippled through her chest and around the crevice. She shrieked with shock, wriggled and fought, yelled and screamed, howled into her mountain hame, felt ill to the pit of her stomach, and then listened as calmly as she could as it cut short, at the

215

same point in the second running each
time . . .

There where the hills are sleeping,
Now feel the blood a-leaping,
High as —

It was almost a relief when the calls
stopped, and she could rest.

★   ★   ★

Sarah had helped deliver a baby once, before
she specialised in intensive care. What had
surprised her was the woman's determination
not to disgrace herself. The woman was
pushing out a kid, screaming for her life,
saying things like, 'You arsehole, get back
here and hold my hand,' but she was
absolutely determined not to mess herself,
and begged the midwife to warn her if this
looked imminent.

Sarah had thought this was slightly
ridiculous. Who cares about anything when
your dignity is so past its use-by date?

Of course, the midwife reassured the
woman that no such thing was imminent as
she secretly whisked away a sanitary pad full
of shit.

But as Sarah lay there, wrapped tightly in

her tent-coffin, she understood. Holding onto your bowels is the last fragment of self-respect and you are programmed not to let go. But the energy and concentration required to hold this in was agonising. Clench, then breathe, count through the pain, hold, clench and breathe. At times there was respite, and Sarah would cry with the relief of it, only to be hurled back into the job at hand. Clench, breathe.

In the end, she was taken unawares when it passed the point of no return, and she cried as she unclenched and unleashed the last scrap of her dignity.

Lying in your own shit is not pleasant. It makes you want to be sick.

Lying in your own shit and vomit is not pleasant. It makes you want to be sick again.

After a hopeless cycle of expulsions Sarah took to breathing tiny little breaths at a time and then stopped noticing the smell and became delirious, chatting to the spider that ran across her face.

'Hello, little one, hello Charlotte. Can you help me? No, you can't, can you? Tell you what, I'm going to push this one with my forehead.'

Sarah started to nudge the rock to her right with her forehead. She pushed, and then rested, pushed, and then rested, and when the blood began to pour down her nose and into her mouth, she licked it and then pushed again before slipping once more into unconsciousness.

*   *   *

What was that?

Sarah could hear something, some talking. A man saying something and a girl laughing.

She found herself saying: 'I'm gonna die I'm gonna die I'm gonna die.' But when Sarah heard her own voice she knew this was a dream because the voice was her six-year-old voice. She was little, and she was rocking back and forth and chanting. The door was locked in this dark place and the voices of the man and the girl outside stopped. This made her panic and she started banging on the dark locked door, over and over again.

'No! Stop! Let me out!'

*   *   *

She woke and felt almost relieved to be in the crevice and not in that other place. She smiled.

'This isn't working, is it? Maybe these tiny little manageable steps work in the Andes, but not in the Highlands. I'm going to make a list of things to do, with some unreasonably big plans. Number one: Let me tell you all about Kyle McGibbon.'

★ ★ ★

Some time later, as she lay amongst spiders in that black scary place, a rat scuttled up her torso and onto her face.

'Hello,' said Sarah with a comical deep voice. 'My name is Sarah.'

Plans and positive thinking and worrying about shit and vomit had faded away long before the rat arrived. Sarah had been lying in a world of swirling daydreams, a world where a little girl was crying and where there was no God. This world was self-contained and almost soothingly dislocated from reality, and it felt like a rude interruption when the rock Sarah's forehead had stained with blood fell to the ground with a thud.

Sarah was afraid. She felt like the little girl in the dark room did all those times when the door was finally unlocked by her stepfather.

Sarah's stepfather was Mike, and he had the most exciting job in the world. He produced movies in Hollywood for years before moving to the UK to work on an exciting new television project. He'd moved to Glasgow after falling for Sarah's mother

— though later Sarah wondered if it was the photo of her five-year-old daughter her mother had carried around with her.

For a year, Sarah was in heaven. Her old dad who'd left her behind was replaced by a sparkling new one, who loved her more than anything and spoiled her rotten. Mike gave her money and sweets and made her the best hot chocolates in the universe. She'd sit at the breakfast bar and watch him heat the milk carefully in a small pot, and then mix the cocoa in a cup with a drop of hot water, and then add the sticky chocolate mixture to the milk and stir it gently. He would then pour it into a large white mug, place it directly in front of her, and watch her smile as he dropped three plump pink marshmallows on top. A wonderful feeling of contentment would wash over her as she watched the marshmallows melt into the warm brown milk.

Mike would also take her to the movies and read to her at night, and babysit when her mum went out and let her watch movies even if they were rated U, and all she had to do for him was invite her friends over a lot and then stay in the en suite like a good girl.

When the rock fell to the ground, Sarah almost said, 'Thank you, Mike,' like she did when he would unlock the en suite door back then, but she'd changed since being buried alive, and manners would henceforth go out the window, so she didn't say thanks or even hello. Sarah must have passed out again, but when she awoke Kyle gave her a drink and popped her shoulder back in with a crunch. He went over her methodically. She could move her arm now, which — amazingly — was otherwise unharmed. She could wriggle her fingers. She could nod that her name was Sarah and that she was in Scotland and that Tony Blair was the Prime Minister of Britain. She could move both legs.

'Your face is swollen, and I think two ribs are cracked . . . But you'll be okay, you're okay.'

Sarah lay there for about sixty minutes with Kyle while he nourished and medicated her and bandaged her ribs. She couldn't talk, didn't want to talk, didn't know what to say, so she sat quietly, looked at the time on Kyle's watch, and regained her strength.

Eventually, she was thinking clearly enough to realise she was sitting on something metal and sharp, a tent peg. And seeing clearly enough to realise that Kyle's bag of goodies included saws and sacks and that he had come to chop her up.

Her fury was so immediate and all-consuming that she pulled the peg from underneath her, sat up, and thrust it through one of Kyle's clear blue eyes and deep into his brain.

He wriggled. He wasn't supposed to wriggle. He was supposed to drop down dead as a doornail. Instead his arms flailed about and he stood up. Sarah didn't have the strength to run after him. So she stood up in her piss and shit-sodden trousers, grabbed another tent peg, and walked after him slowly. He was scrambling pathetically towards the ridge, trying to yelp for help. She had to walk about ten metres before he had slowed down enough for her to catch up. Then he fell to the ground. She looked him in his good eye, and stabbed the metal tent peg right through it.

Sarah pushed Kyle forward and both pegs pressed further into his head with a wet squelch.

It was still dark, so Sarah had enough time to put Kyle's body where she'd spent the last twenty-three hours. She wondered why Kyle had thought he needed to chop her up and take her somewhere else. That was completely unnecessary. No-one was ever going to find a body out here. So after yanking out the pegs and stabbing him in the heart a couple of times, and sawing off both arms so that he would fit neatly into the crevice, she felt sure that he was dead enough to make no fuss, and she shoved him in.

For garnish, she looked inside the crevice and found her spider.

'Hello, Charlotte,' she said as she plucked it from the web it had woven. She then looked at Kyle's face, gently pulled down on his soft bottom lip, prised apart his teeth with her fingers, and popped Charlotte into his mouth.

'This is Kyle, the guy I told you about.'

Sarah set about placing the rocks back. She had overseen the rebuilding of her stone wall in Loch Katrine, so she knew a bit about it, and did a fine job of camouflaging the crevice completely, unlike Krissie who (characteristically) had done a very sloppy job.

She then took off her soiled pants and put on the change of clothes Kyle had packed for himself and mentally ticked off the first of the unrealistically large-scale plans she had made in the darkness.

Kill Kyle.

What luck, him turning up like that. She had imagined that it would take hours to walk to safety and then days to hunt him down, if she had ever managed to free herself from the crevice.

Not only had he showed up like a gift from heaven, but he had fixed her up so that she was strong enough to do him in immediately.

Killing Krissie wasn't going to be part of Sarah's revenge. It wasn't so much that she didn't *want* to kill Krissie — indeed she couldn't believe what her friend had done to her — but a long time ago, Sarah had made a pact with God never to let harm fall upon her friend again.

And anyway, getting Robbie — the child who she felt was rightfully hers — would be vengeance enough.

But how?

When the phone in her pocket rang Sarah was not terrified this time. But she was confused, forgetting momentarily that she could reach into her jacket pocket with her hand, retrieve the phone, and press the button. Easy.

So that's what she did.

'Hello, this is Claire Smith phoning for Sarah McGibbon,' a middle-aged voice said to Sarah. 'I'm a social worker in the Partick area office. I'm ringing about your friend, Krissie Donald.'

30

I'd said my goodbyes to the perfect life I'd thrown to the wind and was about to head down to the police station when the phone rang, startling me.

It was Mum.

'Mum! Where are you? They've taken Robbie into care and I've done something really bad . . . I'm scared. I'm just about to go to the police station.'

Unable to understand my hysterical attempts to explain what had happened, Mum calmed me down a little, then said, 'Darlin', don't do anything yet. Wait till we're with you. Get a taxi to Kenilworth, Kriss. We'll be with you as soon as we can.'

Mum was right, I couldn't do this alone. After she hung up, I longed for her so much it hurt. God, when I thought about all she and Dad had put up with since I'd had Robbie, I felt mortified. They were amazing, and I was a nightmare. And they didn't know the half of it yet.

I moved the broken door aside and stepped out into the close.

I almost fell over Chas, who was sitting on

the step with red eyes that loved me, I knew that now. He'd stuffed up too, and he felt terrible. I apologised for my fury earlier and sat down beside him.

He didn't flinch as I told him about Sarah. When I'd finished, he moved his hand gently onto mine and held it there.

After a period of silence, gazing out the window overlooking the drying green, we got a taxi to Kenilworth Avenue together. I found Mum and Dad's house key in its hiding place in the garage and we went inside. The house was such a happy house. Messy and lived in and happy.

Knowing that in an hour or so I would be removed from this life and from my son, I decided to use the time efficiently, to put things in order so that Robbie would grow up knowing something about his mother that did not involve adultery and murder. I asked Chas to give me some space to do this, so he took himself off to the kitchen to see what he could rustle up. I had not eaten for over twenty-four hours and he was going to force me to, even though it was the last thing I wanted to do.

I took one of Mum's large floral boxes from her creative room. She'd always had this room, filled with pretty boxes, stickers, interesting stationery, books and watercolours. She made stunning little books for Robbie, put together gorgeous photo albums, and kept almost everything in sentimental, accessible order.

I grabbed an empty floral box and labelled it 'Photos for Robbie' with one of Mum's sticky labels.

I rummaged through the loose photos on the desk, downloaded some recent ones from Mum's camera, and put all the shots of me with Robbie inside. On the back of each, I wrote a wee story . . .

Mummy chopping your nails for the first time. They were teensy!

Mummy learning to feed you. She wasn't very good at it!

You and Mummy in the park feeding the ducks. You were asleep!

Gran, Grandpa, Mummy and you eating pasta by Lake Como.

Mummy heading out the door when she was wee — probably to climb trees.

Mummy and her dear friend Sarah . . .

Next I wrote a letter in my best handwriting.

Dear Robbie,

I'm writing this at Gran and Grandpa's. You are on holiday for the night with some new people, and soon you're going to come and live with Gran and Grandpa. I'm going to be away for a while because I've done something very wrong and I need to learn how to make better decisions.

I'm going to miss you so much! I'm so sad I'm not going to see you walk for the first time or sit up at the table by yourself, or head off to the same school I went to. I wish I could, but I want you to know that I will be thinking of you every single day while I'm at the better decisions camp. Every single day, Robbie, and I will be counting down the minutes till I can come home here and live with you and Gran and Grandpa.

I will write to you every day, my little boy!

I love you,
Mummy
xxxx

I was crying by the time I finished. The page was sodden when I sealed it in an envelope.

Then I wrote a letter to Mum and Dad.

Dear Mum and Dad,
I don't know how I've managed to ruin it all. You've done everything right and I've done everything wrong. I know you'll look after Robbie for me, but please don't let

*him forget me. I've been a hopeless mum,
but I love him. And I love you both too,
with all my heart. I'm so, so sorry,*
　Krissie
　xxx

I got another box and filled it with things
that might remind Robbie of me. My
deodorant (it was only Nivea roll-on, but it
was how I smelt), my favourite Enid Blyton
book, the soft bunny I got when I was three,
which I took out a moment later as he was
actually very scary to look at, with evil glass
eyes and re-sewn ears that were tight and too
thin.

I remembered another soft toy, Geoff. He
was a pink teddy bear who I named
controversially because I was an 'interesting'
child. He wasn't in the creative room
anywhere, so I went up to the attic.

Our attic had a pull-down ladder and was
tiny. Dad had put a light up there one rainy
weekend and Mum began to use it to store
things that 'should really be thrown out,
Anna!'

There were several plastic boxes filled with
letters. She's a great writer, Mum. She loves
people — and talks all day about what they
do and say and how they end up being the
way they are.

Mum's letters made wonderful reading.

There were love letters to Dad when he was working in Africa: '133 days till I see you, Davie boy. How am I going to survive without your hand massages and pancakes? Write me with some ways.'

There were letters to me when I was in India. 'You are my golden girl, Krissie. I remember you and Sarah running off to school in the rain and I thought to myself: there go my golden girls with blue umbrellas, running, laughing in the rain.'

And another one from me that Mum had put in a plastic pocket and filed:

Dear Mum,

I am sitting in the branch of a tree in Goa and the sun is setting over the water and it is SO beautiful. I've made friends with a guy from Edinburgh called Chas and have told him all about you. He thinks you sound nice and says I should be better adjusted. I can't stop thinking about home. I miss sitting on the swing at night talking crap and being dragged off for daft weekend breaks.

Kx

PS Don't worry about me. The daftest thing I'm doing is sitting in a rather uncomfortable tree with an asexual Scot.

There was a short story that Mum had written and kept hidden away for years — about a bald boy being bullied on a boat. It was brilliant.

I didn't find Geoff, but I did find two things that really puzzled me. The first was a newspaper clipping about a guy who was fined for a sex offence. He'd managed to reduce the charge, but he was — as the paper put it — a beast on the loose.

BEAST ON THE LOOSE
A paedophile was fined £200 at Glasgow Sheriff Court today for molesting a six-year-old girl. 'He was always a pleasant man,' a neighbour said. 'I still don't believe he did it.' Other residents say they are furious that the man was able to plea bargain his way down to breach of the peace. The offender — who cannot be named — walked away from court this afternoon and has not been seen since.

I had shrugged this off and continued leafing through photos when the second weird thing turned up. Something wrapped in newspaper. I unwrapped the *Observer*, and caught a glimpse of a beautiful jewellery box that was embroidered with pink flowers and encrusted with silver glitter.

Then I threw up all over Mum's letters.

Looking at the box again, I wondered why I had just thrown up. I opened the box slightly, saw the tutu of a tiny ballerina and heard the ping of a mournful tune. To stop myself from throwing up again, I slammed the lid shut, wrapped the box up in the newspaper, and went downstairs to clean Mum's letters.

'What's wrong?' Chas asked when I walked into the kitchen.

'I was looking at a jewellery box in the attic and I threw up.'

Chas's face went whiter than mine, for some reason.

'Do you remember where you got the jewellery box?' he asked.

'No,' I told him, wondering what that had to do with anything.

'Krissie . . . ' Chas was looking very serious indeed, but he didn't get to explain himself because at that moment Mum and Dad rushed into the kitchen and hugged me. They'd been crying, both of them, and asked me to sit down and tell them everything.

So I did. Everything.

How do parents react when their ordinary happy lives somersault and then spontaneously combust?

Mine stayed calm, each taking a turn to ask a question.

'Are you sure it was your fault, Kriss?'

'I pushed her and she fell.'

'But did you mean to?'

'All I know is that I hid her, and that's bad enough.'

'Sometimes I wish you'd never met Sarah,' said Dad.

31

Mum, Dad and Chas sat quietly while I phoned Kyle again. Still no answer. Then Mum phoned Social Services. First, she discovered she'd phoned the department of old and mad people. She was transferred to the bad people section, before a probation officer transferred her again to the young people department, which rang out.

In the end, we drove to the office. Chas and I waited outside nervously for an eternity. When Mum and Dad finally came out, it was to say the social worker was on a child protection investigation. Her mobile wasn't answering and the investigation could go on all day. The receptionist said she'd left a note for me explaining that they hadn't managed to organise a hearing during the day. 'It's at Bell Street, at 6 p.m.,' the receptionist read.

As much as we hated the idea of Robbie being with strangers for the rest of the day, there was nothing we could do.

★　★　★

Dad was silent as he drove us all to Drumgoyne Road. My heart was pounding as we parked at the seventies brick police station. We all sat still, waiting. If I hadn't moved, I think we all would have stayed there forever.

I walked in first, with Chas and Mum and Dad trailing behind me.

'Can I speak to a police officer?' I asked the man on the desk. 'It's urgent.'

I was told to take a seat, which I did, sitting down with Mum, Dad and Chas on one side and several car thieves and prostitutes on the other. They seemed quite at home, reading leaflets on walls and entertaining their kids as if they were at the dentist.

We'd been sitting there for ten minutes when Mum started to cry, so I approached the desk again.

'Excuse me, this is very urgent — ' I looked at his badge — 'Sergeant Gallagher.'

'Aye, I'm sure it is!' said the rude-as-a-bastard police officer. 'Sit down there and we'll call you.'

I sat down again and then Dad started to cry, so I approached the desk again.

'It's about a murder! I killed someone. So please get an officer to take my confession.'

He looked up at me with a different expression. Suddenly I had been promoted from a middle-class bore with a noisy neighbour to a full-blown murderer.

'Oh, right then, of course . . . Um, come in here then, miss.'

I was taken away from Chas's hand and Mum and Dad's (now free-flowing) tears into a little room with glass windows, two inspectors and a tape. Declining a lawyer, I gave as much detail as I could — times, dates, places, affairs, pushes, dislocations — and told them that Kyle was only trying to help me by removing her body.

Within minutes of giving the statement, I was put in a police car. I begged them to bring Chas too, and eventually they relented and let him come in the car behind me. We drove off at high speed to Glencoe, leaving Mum and Dad in Glasgow for the Children's Hearing that evening.

The inspectors were uncharacteristically nice. They didn't call me scum or handcuff me or punch a more interesting confession out of me. In fact, they stopped at Crianlarich and got me some headache tablets.

We parked at the front of the Kingshouse Hotel and as we walked inside I grabbed Chas's hand. It made me nauseous, seeing the hotel where it all started. When Kyle, Sarah and I had arrived here, I was already an adulteress. I had already ruined Sarah's life.

But it was in this building that a blowjob mushroomed out of control.

We walked more slowly up the track than I had the last time I was there, and the only strange thing we saw on the way was an abandoned luggage trolley. We arrived at the top of the mountain at about three in the afternoon. The inspectors followed me to the foot of the cliff and then stood with me in front of the crevice. There was blood everywhere. Had she been bleeding at the time? God, I hadn't even noticed.

The crevice itself was perfectly camouflaged. How had I managed such a good job?

I sat down and looked away while the inspectors photographed the scene and then pulled at the rocks. It seemed to take them forever, and the scraping and banging of rocks was so loud that it felt as though it was happening inside my head. Eventually I heard a thump and the sounds of gagging and then Chas prised my hands away from my tear-sodden face and looked at me calmly.

'Krissie. There's something you need to see.'

32

While Krissie had been confessing to Chas in the close at Gardner Street, Sarah was arriving home in the car Kyle had left at the Kilmore Hotel. She'd managed to drive off without being seen and was in good spirits — in a covered-in-blood-and-shit, mad-as-a-snake kind of way. She found the spare key under the pot plant on the porch and opened the back door of her house.

Sarah had two missions — to get the bastard who'd fucked up her head, and to get Robbie. She had intended to leave Robbie till last, but then she got the call from the social worker, and realised she'd have to rearrange things a little.

Her initial plan to provide Robbie with the love and care he was so clearly lacking would have been a challenge. She'd intended to steal Robbie by snatching him from his cot at night maybe, or better still, from right under Krissie's nose when she had a pee or cleaned her teeth.

After Krissie's controlled crying incident, she'd asked for a key to Krissie's flat ('Just in case!'), so it would have been easy. She could have snuck in, hidden in cupboards and corners and turned on lights and banged doors and scared the shit out of her, then taken the child that was rightfully hers.

But the challenge had been removed, so now all she had to do was meet an old duck at the Partick social work office and take it from there.

Sarah barely noticed the red and brown muck glugging its way down the shower drain. She was thinking hard. The irritating social worker with the nose-ring and the agonising weekend with the ginger runaway and the interminable waiting list had all been worthwhile. Now the social worker would know she was fit to take the boy, because it had been deemed that she was fit, on paper.

Before collecting Robbie, Sarah bandaged her ribs again and tended her wounds. She then packed two large suitcases with all the things that had been denied her on the camping trip — her straightening tongs, her Clarins cleanser and toner, and five pairs of shoes. Almost in a trance, she locked the house and drove to the social work office.

She arrived at the office as it was opening, then waited in reception for five minutes before a beefy woman in her fifties came to the front desk and called her name. They sat for a few minutes in a depressing room that smelt of mental illness and drug addiction. Sarah explained how she'd hurt her head putting up a Safetots baby swing in the backyard and after a brief summary and a few questions, Sarah was given two addresses: one for the foster carer, and one for the Children's Hearing, which she should bring Robbie to that night, at six. The social worker then rushed off on a child protection investigation.

Sarah threw one of the addresses in the bin before she clicked her car door open, and then looked at the other one.

Half an hour later she parked in front of a row of tenements that were boarded up. Opposite were terraced houses. Sarah found number twenty-one and pressed the buzzer. A middle-aged woman opened the door. The woman was a little disturbed by Sarah's scratched forehead and swollen lip, but the social worker had called, so she was expecting Sarah.

Sarah was more than a little disturbed by the woman — did they really allow people with bad teeth and comedy accents to be foster carers? The house had all the trademarks of the underclass — flouncy pink curtains, too many perfectly matched velvet sofas, no doubt required to provide endless hours of comfort to the obligatory unemploy-able husband.

Sarah was bored within two seconds as the woman yakked on about medication and how Robbie slept at two for two hours and then at eight for nine and his favourite mashed veg seemed to be carrot and how his nappy size was a Maxi in Pampers but a Maxi-plus in Huggies.

Before the woman could get properly into how much he'd liked the *Thomas the Tank Engine* DVD she'd shown him, Sarah cut her off with: 'We'll be fine, thanks.' Then she picked him and one of the bags up, and took him to the car.

Just as Sarah realised she had no car seat, the underclass frump walked out with one and strapped it in.

As the Land Rover screeched off, the foster carer realised Sarah had not taken the bag with Robbie's medicine in it.

Sarah decided to go to Perth. No-one would trace her there, and Paul the Sainsbury's man was different. He had listened to her, liked her, thought she was beautiful, and she could trust him. It would be the best place to collect her thoughts and work out the best way to complete the final, most important thing on her list.

It took Sarah over two hours to get to Perth. Normally it would have taken one and a half, but Robbie cried most of the way and this held them up. After half an hour, Sarah stopped the car and cuddled him. When she'd first spotted Robbie in hospital, his eyes had entranced her, spoken to her. They were eyes that loved and understood her.

She looked into Robbie'e eyes now and saw nothing of this understanding and love. They were ugly little screaming eyes and she started to wonder what Krissie had done to the child to make him this way. Her hugging stopped him howling momentarily, but when she took off again he started up with a wail that made her want to drive the car into oncoming traffic.

She started singing to him as she drove:

Train whistle blowin' makes a sleepy noise,
Underneath their blankets go all the girls
    and boys.
Rockin', rollin', ridin' —
What the hell is wrong?
ALL BOUND FOR MORNINGTOWN,
MANY MILES SHUUUUT UUP!

But this approach didn't stop him. The only time he did stop crying was when he projectile puked all over Sarah's Land Rover. A tornado of vomit hit the back of Sarah's head. She screeched into the pretty village of Dunblane and ran into a pub.

'Can I use your bathroom? It's an emergency!'

'There are public toilets at the tourist information office,' said the barman.

Sarah jumped back in the car, where Robbie was screaming at full throttle, and drove round and round the town. Why a small village should have a one-way system and fourteen contradictory signposts she would never understand. Finally, Sarah parked the car at the tourist information office, grabbed Robbie out of the seat, which she now realised required a PhD in physics to do and undo, and ran inside.

'I need the toilets!'

The woman at the counter was talking to someone and asked her to wait a moment, but Sarah interrupted.

'I need the toilets *now!*'

The woman and everyone in the room did some synchronised eyebrow raising and then Sarah saw the toilet sign outside. She ran back out and tried to open the door, but it was locked, so she kicked it a few times and yelled until the frightened assistant came out with the key.

After a makeshift wash, Sarah dried her hair with the hand dryer and looked herself over. She was feeling a little better and she was looking okay. She changed Robbie's

243

clothes and phoned Paul, the Sainsbury's manager, for directions. She then drove off again. Robbie fell asleep and let her drive in peace, and he was still asleep when she arrived in the monoblock driveway of a small semi-detached, newly-built house on the outskirts of Perth. There were hundreds of houses in the street, all the same, all little boxes.

She parked and checked the address. This was no castle.

She knocked on the door and Paul opened it, smiling at her.

'Why did you lie to me?'

'I don't know.'

'You wanted to impress me?'

Sarah had always been chaste and proper, always been respectable. But that was then. In the days before she died and came to life again.

Standing there on the doorstep of his house, she looked at Paul for a second, then knelt, undid his zip, took out his penis and licked it slowly, from top to bottom, in full view of all the little people in all their little boxes. He pulled her to her feet, looking around to see if anyone was watching, and then dragged her inside.

Sarah did not want to have the kind of sex that makes babies. The kind where the man puts his penis into the woman's vagina and ejaculates. She had done this, to no avail, for years.

So when Paul tried to put his penis into her vagina after the wet kiss and the ripping off of clothes, she pushed him off the couch and onto the ground and stood over his head with her legs unashamedly wide apart.

'Just look at me,' she said, and he did, although it got a little boring after two minutes or so. He was about to take the reins and move this thing on when Robbie woke in the car and started to scream.

'What's that?'

'Shit, it's Robbie.'

'Who?'

It's not easy, being a mother, not being able to just do something spontaneous, Sarah thought to herself as she brought Robbie into the house, to discover that Paul the Sainsbury's guy was looking at her very strangely indeed.

'You have a child?' he asked.

'I do now.'

'Do you want a coffee?' he asked, as she put the Pampers Maxi in the bin. 'That'd be great, thanks,' said Sarah, as she fed Robbie some tinned mashed carrot.

'You like it weird, hey?' He was getting excited again. 'You're a dirty little bitch.'

Sarah paused for a moment and held eye contact with Paul. 'Where does this go?' she asked, drying the spoon she had used to feed Robbie his carrot.

He pointed to the cutlery drawer. 'You can't leave me like this, without satisfying me.'

'Sure,' said Sarah. 'I'll just put him in the car.'

She put Robbie back into her Land Rover, angry that — yet again — she had been lied to. Yet again she had been let down. Paul didn't love her, or like her. He thought she was a dirty little bitch. She'd thought Paul was different, but then she'd thought the same about her stepdad and her husband . . . None of them were different, she thought to herself as she came back into the house, her eyes mad, furious.

Paul had his little wobbler waiting, just sitting there pathetically with a drop of piss on its end. He sat on the couch trying to get it hard as she opened the cutlery drawer and put the spoon inside, eyeing a gleaming knife in the section next to the spoons.

She moved over to him and took her pants off.

'As long as you do something for me at the same time,' she said, and then placed herself directly on his face, waiting for him to do what Kyle had started doing that night in the hotel, when she had woken up and walloped him over the head. It felt good, actually.

And she did as Paul had so politely requested, but it was so goddamn boring, and so goddamn irritating when he asked her to lick his hairy balls. After wiping her tongue over the leathery sprouts and digging out a few blackies from her teeth, she brought out the gleaming knife that she had taken from the cutlery drawer and caressed it against his unsuspecting base. She enjoyed moving the sharp edge of the cold blade around and around as her mouth toyed up and down, but then it all seemed a bit clichéd really. She was more imaginative than that. She hid the knife under the sofa and worked on him spectacularly until he was almost ready to go, and then she called upon the skill she had learnt in the crevice, the skill that had seemed like a weakness at the time. She recalled the hours of holding on in excruciating pain, and recalled the blessed release when she unclenched and unleashed the last scrap of her dignity.

Paul's orgasm was nipped in the bud by Sarah's, which was spectacular and multi-coloured.

'Aaagh! Dirty slag!'

Sarah stood up, knife in hand, and nicked him on the leg.

'Aaagh! No! Stop!'

She then held the knife against his neck and squashed her effort into his face, into his mouth, his nose, and his ears.

⋆   ⋆   ⋆

He was still in the bathroom gagging, wiping the sticky excrement from his hair, and scraping out the morsels that had merged with his insides when he heard her car toot its goodbye. The brown saliva spat out from his mouth as he yelled: 'YOU FILTHY BITCH!'

That had gone well, Sarah thought to herself, rubbing her hands with baby wipes. She hadn't got the relaxing rest she had anticipated, but it was invigorating and she felt energetic and inspired enough to complete the last thing on her list.

Kill Mike.

33

Mike bought one litre of milk, the *Times*, a can of tomato soup and three fresh rolls.

'Haven't seen you out running for a while, Mike,' said the shopkeeper.

'I've been too busy getting fat!' said Mike, and they both laughed as he left the shop.

'Morning,' he called, waving to Netty, after crossing the road.

'See you at eight-thirty!' said Netty, who was supervising Isla and her friends as they fashioned a Guy for the bonfire out of rope and newspaper and wood.

The park was a huge success. It had taken days of intense labour, but Mike had organised it beautifully. Before the community knew it, a large wooden boat had materialised in the middle of the grass. Planks and ropes and hidey holes and chutes shot up around and within it, and then kids appeared in droves, buzzing about as their parents and grandparents gossiped happily on the sidelines.

Mike watched the adults whispering on the bench in the park that he had created for them. What were they saying, those ladies and that boring comic man, Jim? And what were they covering in front of the bench? It was something odd, the size of a chair, and badly disguised with an old beach towel.

Mike opened the door to his building, and climbed the stairs to his flat. He read his paper, made some coffee, cleaned the kitchen and then sat at the computer. His office was well organised, with shelving all along one wall, full to the brim with videotapes.

Mike hadn't been to his plot for a week. He had put it out of his mind like a diet gone wrong — it was no longer even a guilty niggle at the back of his mind. The plot, the change of life, the solitude and wholesomeness, it was withering somewhere in Ayrshire.

The plot in Ayrshire was just the last in a string of attempts to change his ways. He'd tried marriage — but the strain of an emotionally appropriate relationship was more than he could take. He'd tried alcohol several times, but this only helped him leap headfirst into his hobby. And he'd considered suicide, but had always chickened out. He wasn't brave enough.

The documentary he was doing about violence in schools was going really well. They had three more days of filming left, and Mike had loads of work to do before tomorrow's shoot. He had to ring the locations manager to make sure everything was okay for the classroom interviews the following day; he had to go over the rushes from the previous day's interviews; and he had to think about Jane Malloy.

First things first. The locations manager assured Mike he'd organised everything for tomorrow, so Mike hung up and moved onto the next thing.

The rushes looked good. There'd been a slashing in the toilets a week earlier, one of many recent slashings of children by children, and Mike had managed a brilliant interview with the ten-year-old victim, Jane Malloy, and her pal, Beth. They spoke lucidly about the ordeal and about what they thought adults should be doing to make things better. Mike had given them twenty pounds each on top of their Channel Four fees, and also a PlayStation game, to thank them for their hard work. Jane's mum was so chuffed with the feedback that she'd happily agreed to bring Jane back for a second interview at his flat the following day.

Which was today.

The rushes gave Mike the rush he was after — those kids in the toilets, that dirty changing room, the pure white flesh of Jane Malloy. It was better than some of the stuff he'd downloaded recently, more immediate, and it was getting harder and harder to find exactly what he was looking for on the internet. There were perverts out there who liked boys, babies even, and sometimes he entered portholes that made him sick to the stomach.

Once or twice he'd procured for the perverts. This had brought problems. There was Marie Johnston's brother, who wouldn't piss off, for instance. He put up with the unpleasantness because the photos traded well.

Mike put his director's hat on as he watched the rushes. If he tried this angle, that, used silk, maybe white, he could not only create hours of entertainment for himself, but also currency, which he could swap with other aficionados.

He had to turn the video and himself off when the doorbell rang.

Jane's mum was typical. Excited by his resume and by his ability to make her daughter a star, she did as every other mum always did. After a coffee, she had no trouble at all buying the old line that the director would be there any minute and that Jane would interview better if she was left alone for a couple of hours.

So when Jane's mum left, Mike played out

the routine he had learnt and practised since he was in his twenties. He'd been in Los Angeles at the time — a high-flier even then — when he started to realise that it was no longer normal to be attracted to children, since he was by then a fully fledged adult.

But there had been fewer restrictions on his behaviour in Los Angeles. No role models — his parents had been dead since he was a baby, and all his in-the-business friends snorted coke and fucked whatever the hell they wanted to fuck. He would never have told his director and actor mates that he preferred girls under twelve, but if he had, they probably wouldn't have batted an eyelid.

He left LA when one kid's mum started making accusations. Since then, he'd zigzagged around the UK. First he lived in London, where his recreational activities were regular and wonderful. Just thinking about a nine-year-old extra from series one of his sitcom made him itch, and when he visualised the girl he met at the park, sitting exactly as he asked in the bushes, it was almost painful.

Then he moved to Glasgow to be with Vivienne Morgan and her beautiful daughter, Sarah. But then Marie Johnston, a pal of Sarah's, squealed to her mum.

He'd misjudged. The money and the soft toys weren't enough. He went to court, and her little brother corroborated, but his lawyer got the charge down to a nice vague breach of the peace.

In those days, they didn't watch out for sex offenders like they do now. There was no registering with the police, nothing, so he simply moved back to London and started over again. But some nutcase found out about him, so he headed north to Drymlee, a quaint family-friendly village thirty minutes from Glasgow, which was far enough for him to avoid any unwanted confrontations with past acquaintances.

He was so pleased with Jane. She was pureness exemplified. He loved that she was giggling flirtatiously on the sofa while he made a pretend phone call to the director who he pretended could not come, and then did a pretend interview about the slashings which she could tell her mum about. Then he went into the kitchen and made some preparations and rubbed himself against the stainless steel fridge a few times while he decided if he should fight it. Everything was going so well for him — his job and his flat and his park and his old-dear neighbour with plants and a granddaughter — and he had been so careful over the last few months.

What the hell, he thought as he downed the rest of his whisky and picked a blank tape from his office, he deserved it. Today, he would spill the Ribena.

34

'Chas, don't make me look, please.'

But the gentleness of his hand and then the expression on his face made me stand up and follow him to the opening.

It was dark in the shadow of the cliff, and for a moment I couldn't see anything but black. I moved closer, dreading the sight of Sarah, the best friend I'd killed and left in this place. I was closer now, my head in the darkness, my eyes adjusting slowly to the black, something coming into view now, something white, red . . .

'Krissie! Krissie, wake up! Krissie, can you hear me?'

Chas and one of the inspectors swirled into view above me and the huge sky was blue and innocent for the brief moment between unconsciousness and reality.

I sat bolt upright.

'Jesus. What? How?'

From the look on the inspectors' faces, we all felt the same; we all wanted to scream in horror at the bath of blood the body swam in, at the open mouth where a three-inch spider was propped on its perfect web, at the sinews of flesh that dribbled from the severed arms, and at the gouged-out eyes of Doctor Kyle McGibbon.

It took Chas a while to convince me that I hadn't killed Kyle, because I just couldn't get my head around it. How else could Kyle be in the crevice? After all, I'd been mad as an ox ever since that illicit shag. Maybe I'd pushed Kyle, not Sarah? Maybe Sarah wasn't even on the cliff that night?

'Sarah *was* here,' said Chas, pointing me in the direction of the detectives, who were placing an item of women's underwear in a plastic bag.

'Oh God!' the detective said, holding Sarah's soiled pants away from his face between two gloved fingers.

★   ★   ★

The police investigation kicked into action with the arrival of the chief inspector. I sat and watched as they sniffed and brushed before moving us back to the place where it had all begun: the Kingshouse Hotel — where we had watched Germany beat England, where I had lain underneath Kyle's thrusting body, and where I had run off into the darkness, mortified that

Sarah was right, that I was unworthy and undeserving of motherhood.

The police set up in the hotel, lining up everyone in chairs in the foyer to be interviewed in turn. I looked around me. The only person I remembered properly was the blonde waitress who had been snogging Matt on the dance floor the night it all started. And that made me think.

Matt. He was there when I walked away that morning. He'd said something — he'd better watch out, what goes around comes around. He had forced himself on me. He had looked at me with evil eyes in Inverarnan and in this very hotel. He had stalked us. Perhaps he had killed Kyle. Perhaps he was so sexually deviant that he had taken Sarah's dead body, and ... Oh my god, what had he done with Sarah's body?

I rushed into the interview room and told them about Matt and then listened as the inspector radioed Highland headquarters.

'We're looking for a twenty-five-year-old man, blue eyes, blond matted hair, hiking gear, with a LOVE tattoo on his upper left arm, very large hands, carrying a red tent on his grey-blue rucksack, probably dressed in khaki shorts and a bright yellow T-shirt that says I AM NOT GAY! in black italic lettering.'

The radio crackled an irregular whoosh: 'Could you be more specific?' the voice sniggered.

I waited in the bar while the rest of the hotel staff were questioned one at a time. They all looked at me suspiciously, especially the blonde waitress Matt had been with. Not just suspiciously, but angrily, as if to say 'Maniac-murderer-bitch!'

The waitress's interview seemed to be interminable but eventually the door opened. It wasn't the waitress who emerged, though; it was the inspectors — and they did not call in the next hotel worker, they walked directly over to me. What were they going to say? They had found Matt? Arrested him? Would they say he had confessed to other murders as well? That he had taken Sarah's body to his damp little cellar to make a set of coffee mugs out of her femurs?

One of the officers ushered me into the makeshift interview room and sat me down next to Matt's waitress bird.

'Krissie, you'll be charged with assault. Maybe attempting to pervert the course of justice. But you're not a suspect.'

'You found Matt,' I said, nodding.
'No, Matt's not guilty of anything.'
'What are you talking about?'
'Sarah McGibbon . . . '
'Yes?'
'Sarah McGibbon is alive.'

35

I rang Mum and Dad. The hearing was at six and if we hurried I would make it. Sarah was alive. I had not killed her. She had left small bloody footprints along the heather, which strongly suggested she had killed her husband and fled the scene. And if more evidence was needed, it was available, because the cute waitress Matt had been with saw her run down the trail like a mad ghost in men's clothing and get in the black four-wheel drive that had arrived in the middle of the night. The cute girl had been bemused and had told several of her colleagues about it over lunch.

But Kyle was dead because of me. If I hadn't gone down on him in the tent, hadn't slept with him in the hotel, hadn't pushed Sarah off the cliff, Kyle would be alive. I had sent him to his grave.

At the same time, I felt elated. I hadn't actually physically *killed* anyone. Thank you, Lord, I said over and over and over again as the hills became farmland became country park became the ugly grey pebble-dashed walls of Glaswegian bungalows. I had not murdered my best friend. I did not have to live with the guilt in a smoky wee room with spookily vacant eyes and bedraggled hair. If given the chance, I could try to be a good mother to my child.

It took a while to persuade the police to let me go to the hearing, for I was a material witness and there were questions to be answered. 'Please,' I said. 'He's sick and he'll be crying . . . Let me go to the Children's Hearing. It'll only take half an hour. Then my parents can look after him till you're finished with me.'

They relented on the condition they escort me there.

As we approached the Children's Hearing, I ran things over in my head. The pros, as the panel would see it, for me keeping my son were as follows:

I was the child's mother.

I would fill the rest in later . . .

★　★　★

The cons for me keeping my child would be:

I was suffering from postnatal depression.

I was an alcoholic.

I had a history of drug use.

I had left the child alone on two occasions.

I was the neighbourhood — hell, the country's — slut.

I was an adulteress.

I had pushed my best friend over the edge of a cliff and then left her for dead, hidden in a cave.

★ ★ ★

I had to be optimistic, I told myself. So, optimistically, I added: But it was all a mistake.

If I were writing a report for the Children's Hearing on myself, it wouldn't be good. In fact, it would be downright bad. I would use sentences like:

Ms Donald seems unable to prioritise her child within her chaotic lifestyle.

There is little evidence to show that Ms Donald can provide consistent and secure care for her son.

Ms Donald showed no insight into her own behaviour and the impact that this behaviour might have on her child.

The writer has little confidence that Ms Donald can work with the department to improve her parenting skills . . .

'Look at me, Kriss.' It was Chas, trying to calm me down. 'You've made mistakes, but you're a good person and we'll work everything out. Just tell them how you feel.'

With the police car waiting outside, I ran

into the building with Chas and one of the detectives in tow. 'You stay here,' I said to Chas, and then went inside and took my seat at that awful table again. The twenty-eight-year-old-arse-with-cowlick who'd accused me (rightly) of being judgmental months earlier, sat opposite me with two other panel members. Mum, Dad and Ms Twin-set and Pearls Social Worker sat next to me, and the reporter sat at the end. They were here to review the child protection order, the reporter said, and to make a decision about what is best for the child. Did I have anything to say?

'Yes,' I coughed. The word stuck in my throat; no arrogance, no aggression. I did have some things to say.

First, I wanted to apologise for the mistakes I had made — for leaving Robbie alone, drinking slightly too much, working too hard, and — I looked at the guy with the cowlick — for being judgmental in the past. Being a mother is the hardest thing in the world, I said. I'd never realised how hard.

Then I begged for help. I would see a counsellor, stop drinking, live with Mum and Dad, take my medication, anything. 'But please, please,' I begged, 'let me be the one to look after him.'

Pearls spoke for too long in the local social work dialect called Jargonish, which left the three panel members to make their decisions like reality talent show judges.

'I have made my decision and . . . '

Long pause.

' . . . And I would like to recommend that the child be returned to the mother, with some voluntary social work support, to get her on track again.'

An identical recommendation followed, before it was the arse-with-cowlick's turn. He looked at me for the first time since that hearing fourteen months before and said, with surprising tenderness, 'That's unanimous. Robbie should be with his mother.'

I was so happy I could have hugged him, that little softy who was doing a good decent job and not getting paid, and I was almost about to when the reporter at the end of the table said, 'You can collect Robbie from your friend whenever you like.'

'What?'

'Your friend, Sarah McGibbon.'

'*Sarah McGibbon?*'

'She picked him up from the foster carer first thing this morning.'

36

I hyperventilated all the way to Sarah's house. She had been cheated on, lied to, assaulted and buried alive. She had gouged out her husband's eyes and sawn off his arms. And now she had Robbie. What would she do next? What would she do with my little boy?

Maybe nothing, I told myself. Maybe nothing. Maybe she would look after him, love him. After all, a baby was all she'd ever wanted.

'His medicine!' I said. 'Check if she took his medicine!' If she took Robbie's antibiotics and paracetamol, I figured, then in her own fucked-up way it would show that she still had Robbie's best interests at heart.

Everyone got on the job of trying to find out if Sarah had taken Robbie's medicine from the foster parents. After twelve phone calls and seven minutes we discovered that she hadn't.

Oh God, I thought to myself, she has no intention of looking after him.

★　★　★

The storm doors to Sarah's sandstone semi were locked. There were no lights on, and there was no car in the driveway. I opened the car door before we'd even stopped and sprinted over to where the spare key was kept. It was gone, so the police kicked in the door. There was no-one in. I checked every room, but each one seemed emptier than the last, none more so than the nursery Sarah had meticulously decorated. Tiny Tears, twenty-nine years old but still in pristine condition, was lying in the cot.

I jumped back in the police car and the siren went on. Where could she have gone?

Her mother's?

Her father's?

Loch Katrine?

The airport?

We sped back the way we had come, screeching to a halt outside Sarah's mother's building.

I ran out and pressed the button that said Morgan.

There was no answer.

'Shit.' I tried again.

No luck. A third attempt . . .

'Yes?' The voice I wanted to hear.

'Mrs Morgan, it's Krissie Donald.'

'Krissie! Hello.'

'I need to come in. It's urgent.'

The buzzer sounded and I bolted up the stairs to the third floor.

She opened the door calmly.

'Is Sarah here?'

'No.'

'Have you heard from her?'

'No.'

'Listen, Kyle's dead, and she's gone off with my baby.'

'Oh dear Lord!' she said. 'Why me? That girl! Will I never have peace?'

I had no patience for her self-obsessed melodrama. 'Mrs Morgan, you have to call 999 immediately if you see her!'

The police took calls as we drove. Another policeman radioed to tell us Sarah's dad was lying drunk in his council flat and had not seen her since he'd asked her for money two years earlier. 'Tight-arsed bitch,' he'd said, apparently, before pouring himself another Buckfast.

She hadn't tried to leave the country, police headquarters informed us. They'd checked the airports.

She'd withdrawn money in Glasgow around 8.30 a.m., but had not used any credit cards.

It took us forty minutes to get to Loch Katrine and when we did the local police had already checked the house. Though they'd seen no sign of Sarah having been there recently, they did want to show us something.

A police officer was waiting at the front door. 'No one's been here for a while by the looks, but come in and check this out.'

I followed the police officer into the master bedroom, where he stopped in front of a tipped-over cupboard. Behind it was a dusty alcove-room.

There's always one, isn't there, in stories about mad people? Locked rooms with bad lighting and pictures and clippings all over the wall. Only the pictures are usually of potential victims and the clippings are of casualties. In this case, as the single bulb swung, pictures of a smiling face came into view.

The man getting an award in LA.

Getting into his car in London.

Getting married in Glasgow.

Getting reviewed in the *Guardian*.

Getting out of hospital in Islington.

All the photos had been scribbled on with angry black pen.

And the man in question — Mike Tetherton.

'That's Sarah's stepdad,' I said.

Chas walked into the room and saw the pictures. His face changed and his whole body went stiff.

'I don't understand,' I said, panicking because it seemed we had run out of leads to find Robbie. Mike Tetherton hadn't been part of Sarah's life since she was six. She'd never mentioned him and hadn't even invited him to her wedding.

Chas led me to the living room and sat me down on the sofa. 'Mike Tetherton is the man I assaulted,' he said.

'What? What's that got to do with anything? We need to find Robbie.'

'Remember when you vomited in your mum's attic?'

'When I was looking at the jewellery box?'

'Sarah's stepdad gave it to you.'

He was looking at me intensely, waiting to see something in my eyes, and initially it confused me. Then he said, 'When you were six, Krissie.'

It was such an innocent thing in itself, the box, embroidered pink flowers encrusted with silver glitter. Such a pretty thing, the white ballerina. Such a lovely tune, 'Doctor Zhivago', pinging out mournfully.

Tears shuddered out of me as my eyes filled with the memory.

I had never bought all that stuff about repressed memories and I used to hate social workers who went on and on about it. The idea that people could bury stuff in their minds and just forget had seemed ridiculous. Real experiences couldn't be brought back to the surface by a smell or a sound or an object.

I was wrong. It was like a whole piece of my life flew into the window, smashed through the glass, and fell down dead at my feet. There it was. Very sudden, very distressing, and very ugly.

He was so nice, Mike, I remembered. I used to beg to go to Sarah's and play because we got crisps whenever we wanted and even watched *Prisoner Cell Block H* once, which my dad had banned because it was 'that bloody lesbian show'. And even after the first time, when we went to the guest bedroom to read some of Mike's Noddy books, and Sarah went into the en suite for a pee, and even after he accidentally spilled a glass of Ribena on me and took my clothes off to dry me with a towel, even after this first time, I still wanted to play there more than anywhere else in the whole world.

It was only after the next time, when there were no crisps and no Ribena and no Noddy books that I started to change my mind. Sarah went in for a pee again, and as I had no goodies to distract me, I noticed that he locked the door of the en suite from the outside and the door of the bedroom from the inside and that he did not talk with his sweet smooth voice but with a hard one that said: 'Just lie there and be quiet.'

The guest bedroom was filled with toys. The guest bed was so pretty, with a fluffy pink and mauve patch-work quilt. There was a video recorder set up in the corner. He was a man, but he seemed to like pink and mauve and Noddy and Big Ears. I didn't think any of this was unusual at the time; a six-year-old doesn't.

I did think to ask him if I would get any crisps and he said only if I lay down and kept quiet. So I did, and afterwards I not only got crisps but the most glorious jewellery box I had ever seen.

Mum almost forced me to have a sleepover at Sarah's not long after. She had been called into work, and was annoyed with me for having a tantrum and making her life hard.

An hour after Mike had generously sent his wife off for a night out with the girls, I could hear Sarah banging on the door of the en suite but not helping me.

Afterwards I was surprised at the re-emergence of his lovely honey-gravel voice.

'She and Sarah played Twister. I'm afraid her wee leg got a bruising,' he said when Mum picked me up.

One more time after that, and some blood

which kept on coming so I had to make up a story about falling off my bike, and then I wrapped up Mike Tetherton and his hard bit and put them away and never thought about him again until Loch Katrine.

* * *

I was still crying when Chas explained about the newspaper article in the attic. It was about Marie Johnston. She'd been there too, positioned in front of that camera, that recorder, the little blossom. She had told her mum, but he'd got away with it.

Chas told me gently that that was why my mum let it lie. She didn't want me to go through what Marie had gone through. What was the point? Marie had been examined by social workers and doctors and police and her mum had refused to let her out to play for weeks on end and her father told her never to wear skirts again and she and her brother became weird at school and no-one wanted to play with them.

I realised that was why Sarah had always watched out for me while I counted bricks at Central Station, why she gave me money when I needed it through uni, why she made freezable meals for me, why she took me on the West Highland Way. She had protected me ever since, because she hadn't been able to when we were little.

I looked at Chas sitting beside me on the sofa.

'Stop!' I said, coming back to the real world at last. 'There's no time for this.'

'But don't you see?' Chas said. 'She's getting revenge — killing Kyle, stealing Robbie — it's like a list of things to do . . . '

I finished Chas's sentence for him: 'She's going to get Mike Tetherton.'

37

After Anna had told Chas about Mike Tetherton, she begged him to let it lie. There was no evidence, and Krissie had been through enough. She was happy, not remembering, so it was best left alone. Anna had been over and over it in her head, and had spent most of her life trying to stop her husband from killing the bastard.

Chas promised he would say nothing. He promised he would give Krissie time, so he left Scotland before he changed his mind.

When Chas arrived back home six years later, he spent two weeks setting up his flat and his studio before going to see Krissie. He'd wanted to impress her, blow her away with his paintings and his new hairdo and his anecdotes.

Chas now knew he was desirable because women had been chasing him over the previous three years; every place he went there was a woman who wanted him. He didn't often resist, because he liked sex just about more than anything, but he never took it further than a week or two. He was in love, he told them, one after another, and their faces fell with disappointment when he admitted it was not them he was in love with, but an amazing woman back home in Glasgow called Krissie.

After cleaning his new flat, ironing his new sheets and hanging the portrait of Krissie that had made him cry when he painted it in Pokhara, Chas arrived at Krissie's flat in his best smart-casual Firetrap jeans and grey-green Billabong T-shirt, with flowers and chocolates and a speech.

'Krissie Donald, I am in love with you and have been since you ate with your hands in Goa. You are wonderful and clever and funny and beautiful and enchanting and I want to spend the rest of the day with you.'

He hoped she would then say: 'Day?'

And that he would then say: 'Okay, then, life. I want to spend the rest of my life with you.'

He rang the bell again and began to rewrite his speech. Too many adjectives. He took out wonderful and changed clever to intelligent and beautiful to gorgeous and then put wonderful back in and took out gorgeous. He also started to sweat through the grey bit of his grey-green T-shirt and wondered if he should wipe his underarms with some of the tissue from around the lilies.

He was tearing off some of the tissue paper

when the door opened at long last.

He breathed in.

But it wasn't Krissie. It was a huge, hairy, half-naked, brown-eyed Adonis.

'Fuck.'

Yes, he had said this out loud.

'Fuck to you too,' said Adonis.

'Sorry.'

'Are those for me?' Shit, as well as being a Greek god, Adonis was funny.

'No.'

There was a pause as the guy looked at the tears welling in Chas's pathetic eyes.

'You're after Krissie.'

'I was.'

'Listen,' Adonis whispered. 'Don't be upset. It's nothing serious. I'm married. So if you want her, she's yours, but leave it a bit, till I've told her.'

Before Chas could regret the pain of breaking his hand on the brick-like chest of Adonis, Krissie appeared behind him.

'Chas!' She grabbed him and hugged him and looked at the flowers and chocolates.

'These are for you — a hello present,' he said.

'Thanks!' she said, taking them without even thinking for a moment that they were supposed to signal the beginning of true happiness for both of them.

'Come in! How have you been? Tell me everything! Why didn't you write?'

Chas insisted that he would not come in, and they talked at the door awkwardly while Adonis waggled his fantastic bum into the bathroom.

'He's the love of my life,' said Krissie. 'I have never ever felt this way before. Did you see that bum?'

'I've got to go,' said Chas.

'Oy, ya stroppy git,' Krissie protested as he walked away. 'Come back and have a cup of coffee. Chas! Get back here.'

'Some other time.'

Chas would have avoided jail had he not babysat for his nephew that evening. The wee one, Joey, wouldn't sleep, so they lay on the sofa together and watched endless amounts of mind-numbingly boring children's television. One of the shows was *The Book Worm*, which featured a travelling library, a large talking/driving worm, and dozens of singing kids in various locations around the UK. Chas and his nephew were almost asleep when the credits rolled, and the producer's name — Mike Tetherton — filled the screen.

Chas rang Anna, and they rang the police and waited days and days until they were told that nothing could be done. Mr Tetherton was not working with children anymore as the show had not been recommissioned, and he was not a registered sex offender.

The following night Chas was fast-forwarding and rewinding *The Book Worm* angrily, watching the faces of the little girls in the show — happy? scared? sore? — when Krissie knocked on his door crying.

'He's married!' she said.

They drank two bottles of wine between them. Chas finally had his arm around her on the sofa and it felt so very comfortable. This was it, this was the moment he had been waiting for, when Krissie would allow herself to be loved by someone who actually liked her.

'Krissie . . . '

'Yep?'

A pause.

'Krissie Donald . . . '

Krissie looked puzzled as she waited for Chas to get another word out; then her mobile rang.

She listened, then hung up, and then it rang again and she listened and did not hang up, and her arm withdrew from Chas's and she went all gooey and soft, and then put her coat on, giggling, and — while still on the phone — mouthed the crushing words: 'Got to go.'

After the second bottle of vodka was

squeezed of its last drip, Chas boarded the train to London. He didn't really know what he was going to do. Yell at him? Talk some sense into him? Catch him at it?

He rang the BBC the next day and said he was the father of one of the girls in *The Book Worm* who was hoping for more work. The BBC receptionist said she'd pass on the message.

Mike called the mobile number as soon as he got the message, and agreed to meet father and daughter at his flat to discuss. By the time Chas got to the flat, he was hungover and exhausted. Mike opened the door with a smile.

'Mr Worthington?'

'Yes, hello,' said Chas, and then explained nervously that his daughter was at school, but that she would love to do some more acting work.

Chas sat down as Mike made a coffee and said he would have to see her again, audition her. Chas checked the place out with his eyes — trendy, neat, bedroom door shut.

'You live alone?' Chas asked.

'Recently dumped! So describe your daughter to me, I can't recall her.'

'Okay, let me think, she has . . . brown hair, she's funny, with a wonderful smile. She's beautiful looking, has a great Scottish accent.'

'From Scotland?'

'Glasgow. Southside.'

'Really?'

'Yes.'

Mike walked in with the coffees and sat down.

'Tell me more.'

'Let me think, she's clever, and she's . . . scared, doesn't let anyone love her. Her name is Krissie Donald, and she is the best friend of your former stepdaughter, Sarah. Do you remember her now?'

The honey-gravel turned to pure granite. 'Who are you?'

Chas stood up and walked towards the bedroom. He'd read about paedophiles, knew what to look out for in their houses — kiddy traps like toys and sweets, premeditated practicalities like doors that would not usually require a lock.

'Why do you have a lock on the bedroom door?'

'Get out or I will call the police.'

Chas moved inside the bedroom.

'Okay, ring them, and put me on when you're done.'

Chas lifted up one of the many teddy bears on the bed. 'Why do you have all these teddies? This bed?'

Mike had turned bright red. 'What do you want?'

'What I really want is to kill you, but that would fuck up my life, and I don't want to do that, so instead I'll settle for a full confession.'

Chas pressed record on the dictaphone he'd purchased that day in Kensington.

Mike left the bedroom, grabbed his keys, and walked out of the flat.

Chas followed him out the front door and onto the street.

'He's a paedophile!'

Chas stayed one step behind him. People turned and looked, and one woman, who had just smiled at her ever-helpful neighbour, seemed puzzled and annoyed when Chas yelled at her: 'He's a beast.'

Mike's pace picked up and he was almost running when he reached the Tesco car park, which was full of shoppers.

'Admit what you've done, here, in front of these people. Say it!'

People stopped in their tracks as Mike stopped walking, turned around and looked Chas in the eye. He stood still for a moment and looked as though he was ready to talk, the dictaphone recording with a hiss. He then whispered, 'So that was her name.'

Mike grabbed a shopping trolley and pushed it against Chas to stop him from reacting. He stood triumphant as the crowd dissipated, then walked away and disappeared into an underground station.

Chas grabbed the trolley to get it out of the way. The trolley was broken, and a metal bar came loose in his hand. He looked at the jagged bar, gripped it tight, and then ran down the stairs of the underground to commit an act that would lose him the next four years of his life.

If only Chas's solution had worked. Kill the bastard.

But unfortunately it didn't.

Instead, Chas turned an angry child rapist into an angrier child rapist.

At the Old Bailey, Chas kept his mouth shut. He knew Krissie wasn't ready to deal with it, and so, as far as anyone but Krissie's parents knew, Mike Tetherton was the unfortunate victim of a dope-smoking drop-out.

Mike moved north and disappeared for a while into a sea of skipping ropes.

38

Sarah had no idea that if she drove fast enough she could be the heroine, the woman who might save the victims from the madman just in the nick of time. As she drove with earplugs in to stop the noise of the kid, who seemed possibly the most difficult kid on the planet, she had no idea that a girl was crying as she lay on a pink and mauve patchwork quilt.

But she was not going to be the heroine of this story and she did not get there just in the nick of time because she was crawling past traffic cones ten miles north of Drymlee when Jane said, 'Thank you very much, Mr Tetherton,' and got into her mum's car with a sweetie necklace that would leave a strange taste in her mouth for the rest of her life.

When Sarah arrived in Drymlee, the little boy in the back of her car sat quietly, no longer trying to get attention by crying. He was burning hot and so exhausted that he just stared vacantly ahead through glassy eyes.

Sarah expected to find Mike straight away. The village was tiny, and very pretty, but she couldn't at first find Wilkinson Court, where he was renting an attic conversion.

She stopped the car opposite a lovely play park to check her map. A huge unlit bonfire, topped with a man made of wood and paper, sat in the corner of the park. The map told her she was right in front of Mike's building. It was gorgeous, made of stone, and on three levels, with at least six flats.

Sarah looked at the building for some time, taking it in, and then started the car and hunted for two hours for the equipment that she needed.

* * *

Sarah's revenge was an all-consuming and passionate affair, which she had nurtured for years and polished in the cave. It was within reach now. Her words and actions were rehearsed to award-winning standards. So close.

Yet when Mike answered the door with his warm, welcoming smile, she felt none of the elation she'd imagined she'd feel. She felt flat and confused, and the script and stage directions she had memorised went completely to pot.

What she was supposed to do after he answered with a welcoming smile was say: 'Mike Tetherton, you have ruined my life and you do not deserve to live.'

She would then hit him over the head with the large rock she had found for this purpose in the park near the fishing shop and, while he was unconscious, she would drag him to the bed and tie him to it. She would search the flat for the images he'd downloaded, and the tapes he'd made of the little girls over the years, and carefully line them up beside the bed.

When Mike woke, Sarah would stand over him and continue her speech.

'Mike Tetherton, you have also ruined Krissie Donald's life, Marie Johnston's life, and — ' pointing to the videos — 'the lives of all these girls, and you do not deserve to die peacefully.'

She would then bring out the kitchen knife she'd cherished since Perth, and make a one-inch incision into his thigh. He would wince and cry like a baby but she would be undeterred.

She would slowly bring out the bag of maggots she had bought at the fishing shop and hold one between her fingers. It would wriggle madly and she would continue: 'This little fella is just like you. He likes to feed on flesh. He wriggles into you and begins to eat. He burrows and grows, burrows and grows, and stays in there for a long, long time.

Eventually, he turns into something else, something too big, something that needs to fly.'

She would then hold up one of the pornographic images from his collection, of a little girl called Miranda or Julie or (insert name as appropriate), and place the maggot into the incision in his thigh.

'This one's for Miranda.'

Sarah would make at least fifty incisions, all around his body, and watch him wriggle and scream as he was colonised.

It was a very satisfying plan, one that worked on every level.

But when Mike answered the door, Sarah went numb and then began to get it all wrong: 'Hello, Mike,' she said, with no speech, no rock and no fall to the ground. 'Do you remember me? I'm Sarah, Sarah McGibbon — I mean Morgan.'

'Sarah? Of course. Are you all right?'

'No, I'm not all right actually. I've had a very bad week.'

'Come in. Who's this?'

'This is Krissie's little boy, Robbie. I've taken him. I suppose I shouldn't have, really.'

'He's boiling!' Mike said. 'He needs Calpol!'

Not surprisingly, Mike had every child-calming remedy and treat on the market, including Calpol, which he gave to Robbie carefully. He then put Robbie on the sofa, looked through Sarah's bag and got some formula, which he mixed and warmed and then gave to Sarah to feed him.

Next he began to warm some milk in a small pot on the cooker. After Robbie fell asleep, Sarah put him down on the bed and walked over to the breakfast bar to watch Mike. She felt warm as he put some cocoa into a small cup, boiled the kettle and then added a drop of water to the cocoa.

'Why are you here, Sarah?' he asked as he stirred the cocoa into a sticky mixture, and then added it to the small pot of milk.

She was so confused now. He was lovely. Her stepdad, Mike.

'I'm here to kill you. I'm going to tie you to the bed and put maggots in your body and then I'm going to give all your photos and downloads and videos to the police.'

Mike poured the milk into a large white mug and put it in front of her and laughed. 'That's very dramatic!'

Sarah held up the bag of maggots weakly and placed them on the breakfast bar. She then placed the large knife beside it. She had lost all her strength, was practically dead with the exhaustion of it all, and knew what she was saying sounded completely ridiculous.

Mike walked out of the kitchen and into his bedroom. Sarah could hear a drawer open and close.

'Wouldn't it be easier to use something like this?' Mike asked when he reappeared a moment later with a SIG .45 handgun. He put the gun on the bench in front of Sarah. 'It's loaded.'

Sarah looked at the gun. Mike was standing opposite her at the breakfast bar.

Sarah touched the gun. It was icy cold and her trembling fingers left patches of condensation on it. Mike had not moved. There was no noise, just the trickling of a tap that needed a washer, the distant hum of a crowd gathering in the park outside, and the breathing of two people.

She picked it up and held it. It was heavier than she anticipated.

Mike's eyes froze. He hadn't expected her to pick it up.

Sarah then stood suddenly and extended her arm, the gun firm in her hand, mere inches from Mike's face.

She placed her finger on the trigger, watched herself press on it. But her hand began to shake. Slight shakes at first, and then large involuntary ones, like a seizure. She closed her eyes to focus, and felt skin. Warm, tender skin. Opening her eyes she saw that Mike's hand was on hers. He was looking at her.

She looked back into eyes that were wet, compassionate; eyes that loved her.

Mike helped her put the gun back down. His hand rested on hers for a moment on the bench, both of them clasped over the gun, and then, nonchalantly, he removed his hand, took three plump pink marshmallows from a jar, and plopped them into the steaming milk.

Sarah looked at the marshmallows as they melted, then looked up at his rugged handsome face and his relaxed pose. He had his honey-gravel voice on now, and she loved it.

'Why didn't you want me anymore?' she asked.

'Sorry?'

'Why didn't you want *me*? What did I do wrong?'

'I'm a sick man, Sarah. I hate what I do. I want so badly to change,' said Mike, touching the gun on the bench. 'Sometimes I think I should kill myself. End it. Wouldn't that be a good idea? To end the pain? To be free of all the worries and all the guilt? But I'm not brave enough.'

Mike touched Sarah's hand tenderly.

Sarah looked up at him, needy, desperate,

and said: 'I didn't help my friend, I didn't help Krissie.'

'Sarah, you were five . . . '

'Six.'

'You were six-years-old. A child. You were locked in a room, and you couldn't have done anything. I think you were very brave, actually, a very brave girl. I'm not brave like that.' Mike indicated the gun again.

Sarah started to sob and Mike sat beside her at the breakfast bar and held her in his arms.

'It's all right, it's going to be all right. You've always been brave, Sarah, that's what I love about you.'

She wet his shirt with her tears, and took in the warmth of his body, the kindness of his arms.

After she'd finished crying, he took her chin in his hands and whispered: 'Sarah, darling, I'm going to make sure Robbie's safe in the bedroom, and then I'm going to leave. Okay? In an hour I'll make a call to social services to let them know he's here, to make sure he's all right, then everyone will be okay.'

'Okay,' said Sarah.

Mike handed her the gun. 'Why don't you take this into the en suite, like a good girl?'

Sarah did as she was told. She went into the en suite and sat on the cold tiled floor.

Mike didn't lock the door from the outside like he used to, and she wondered why. She could hear Mike packing a few things from the kitchen. She toyed with the gun, her future, and then heard Mike come into the bedroom. She opened the door slightly and peeked through the crack.

Robbie was sleeping at last, with just his nappy on.

Mike was packing his tapes into a suitcase, keeping them in order. He shut down his computer, thought for a moment, looked at the nine-month-old baby on the bed before him, and it came to him.

Currency.

It was disgusting, but perverts would do anything for pictures of this one, give him anything. One or two shots and he'd be set up with enough material in his demographic to do him for months.

He sat beside Robbie on the bed and moved him into the middle of the patchwork quilt.

Turning the lights on, he switched on the video camera that was still set up on its bracket in the corner. Then he took his small silver digital camera out of its black leather case and checked it over, smoothed the quilt, and positioned himself near Robbie.

There was noise at the en suite door. A

click, and breathing. Mike turned around and saw her there, standing in the doorway with her pathetic thin shaky fingers on the trigger again.

He smiled. She wouldn't do it; he knew her well enough.

'Move away from him!' she said.

He did not move away. He looked into her eyes again with his camera in his hand. 'Sarah, come on — this is pathetic,' he said.

But this time Sarah did not tremble.

And this time, when Sarah looked into Mike's eyes, she did not see compassion or love. She saw the opposite.

With a firm, determined arm, Sarah checked her positioning and pulled the trigger.

The force of it made her lose her balance, and she fell back against the wall of the en suite and onto the floor.

The force of the bullet sent Mike staggering backwards too, and he smashed his way though the bedroom window and fell twenty metres onto the street below.

39

A group had assembled at Greensleaves for Guy Fawkes night, which was to double as an opening for the park. Netty, Isla, the resident's association treasurer and her four children and several other families from Wilkinson Court stood around the bench in the park. Isla held a blanket over an object the size of a chair with a huge smile on her face.

At the other end of the park, a makeshift Guy stood tall, as yet unharmed by the rising flames of the bonfire beneath it.

Cartoon-shop Jim squatted to the left of the bonfire, waiting for the signal to light the fireworks — Mike's arrival.

Netty had just checked her watch when the gun went off, and she jumped along with the rest of the crowd. They looked to Jim, assuming he had started the fireworks early. He shook his head. There was a moment's silence.

Everything stood still in Greensleaves:

Isla, holding the blanket over the object, desperate to undertake her important duty in the opening ceremony.

Netty, her speech ready.

The little black labrador, his tail wagging, eyes fixed to the front door of his master's house, his tongue out.

Jim, all set to light the fireworks.

And everyone else, hands poised to clap.

They all looked up as the glass of Mike's window shattered. And after the body landed with a thump they ran towards it. When they reached him they stood in a semi-circle and beheld a mouth that was uncharacteristically smirky, eyes that were uncharacteristically hateful, and legs that were uncharacteristically akimbo. In his hand, Mike clutched his silver camera.

Isla had screamed when she heard the body land. She had dropped the blanket, which she was supposed to remove under different circumstances, when Netty finished her glowing speech. Instead, she ran to the thud and the blanket twirled in the wind to reveal, to no-one, a glorious shiny black granite plaque, smack bang in the middle of Greensleaves, that read: TETHERTON PARK.

The puppy, who Mike had never bothered to name, yelped with grief at the loss of his beloved.

And as the Guy at the top of the bonfire finally burst into flames behind them, the residents of Wilkinson Court watched the pup, wishing they could yelp too.

★ ★ ★

In South Ayrshire, a lonesome moonlit deckchair sat incongruously on a plot of land. A gust of wind caused it to wobble slightly and a second gust tipped it over.

40

I was not the hero of this story either. I did not save the day and I did not get there just in the nick of time.

In the police car, I shut my eyes and prayed — or was I begging? Let Robbie be okay. Let Robbie be okay. Let nothing have happened to him. Please.

When we arrived at Wilkinson Court, Mike had been dead for ten minutes. We parked beside a new park that was illuminated by a huge bonfire. Local kids were watching the goings on from the top of a wooden pirate ship.

Mike was lying on the street. I didn't see his face.

I'm glad.

I ran past the gasping/nattering/tearful onlookers, and up to the small flat in the attic.

It was just a flat. Clean, bright. An everyday flat.

I opened the door to the bedroom. Robbie was sleeping comfortably on the bed, not hot or in pain. He had a blanket over him and he looked content.

I kissed him on the cheek and passed him to Chas before looking around the room. Glass was shattered on the floor and the en suite door was shut. It gave me the shivers.

'Sarah!' I said. 'Sarah!'

There was no noise.

I opened the door to the en suite and, when my eyes adjusted to the gloom, I could see the gun on the floor, and I could see that Sarah's face was calm.

I sat down on the tiles with her, the thick blood coating us both, enveloping us in its red warmth, and I hugged her.

As I looked into her eyes I saw the golden girl Mum had written about — we were 'the golden girls with blue umbrellas, laughing, dancing, in the rain'. I saw the girl in the garden, changing Tiny Tears with precision and purpose. I saw the girl at Central Station keeping watch for me, always keeping watch, and the girl saying 'I do' at the altar with a huge, beautiful grin.

And I saw the girl who was never properly loved by anyone, not even by me, in the end.

'Is Robbie all right?' she whispered into my ear.

'He's fine,' I whispered back, holding her as tightly as I could while she slipped away.

41

A few weeks after we moved into Mum and Dad's, I dreamt that a huge pot of sauce was simmering away on a cosy little cooker in an everyday kitchen.

As I moved closer to the bolognese, I could see a man's back. He was stirring the pot, gently stirring away, dispersing that wonderful smell through the room. A feeling came over me as I walked towards the stirrer and hugged him. I didn't recognise it, had never felt it before. And it took me ages to identify it. It was peace, swimming over me. I felt peace.

It was Chas, stirring the sauce, and the feeling that swept through me was so strong and so new that it woke me up.

He woke too, and held me as I soaked in the bolognese feeling that would be mine now forever.

$\star$ $\star$ $\star$

A therapist helped me with an action plan. There were big things and little things, and it was the little things I found the hardest.

Watching Robbie cuddle Tiny Tears.

Posting a letter to Kyle's parents. That was hard.

Visiting Sarah's grave; that, too.

And getting rid of the jewellery box. I threw it out the same day Robbie stood up by himself for a full ten seconds by holding onto the coffee table with his four new teeth. Chas spotted me at the wheelie bin as he walked home from the corner shop with two litres of semi-skimmed milk and four croissants.

* * *

Now I'm sitting here in the darkness of Mum's 'creative room' trying to put Robbie to sleep and he's not complying. I put my face in my hands with exasperation and when I lift up my head I see that Robbie has grabbed my fingers and is holding onto them tightly. At the same time, he is looking me in the eye and laughing. Without even thinking about it, I grab his hand, look him straight in the eye, and laugh right back.

We do hope that you have enjoyed reading this large print book.

Did you know that all of our titles are available for purchase?

We publish a wide range of high quality large print books including:
Romances, Mysteries, Classics
General Fiction
Non Fiction and Westerns

Special interest titles available in large print are:
The Little Oxford Dictionary
Music Book
Song Book
Hymn Book
Service Book

Also available from us courtesy of Oxford University Press:
Young Readers' Dictionary
(large print edition)
Young Readers' Thesaurus
(large print edition)

For further information or a free brochure, please contact us at:
Ulverscroft Large Print Books Ltd.,
The Green, Bradgate Road, Anstey,
Leicester, LE7 7FU, England.
Tel: (00 44) **0116 236 4325**
Fax: (00 44) **0116 234 0205**

BLOOD PRECIOUS

Sara Banerji

Snobbish, aloof and eighty years old, Lady Arabella Cunningham-Smythe wishes she were dead. Then she could join her late husband as they had planned so meticulously before he died. But her well-meaning friends and relations are determined to thwart her wishes. When her beloved four-year-old granddaughter, Naomi, is kidnapped, Arabella's will to live must return if she is to turn detective, successfully outwit a mass murderer — and learn how to use her mobile phone . . . In the hunt for Naomi, she experiences a new intensity of life — and discovers at last who she really is.

LOCKED IN

Peter Conway

Is Father Carey a saint or sinner? Comforter of the sick — or a heavy drinker not to be trusted with secrets, confessional or otherwise? Opinion at St Cuthbert's Hospital is divided. Michael Donovan, paralysed after a rugby accident, views him as the only person to give him support. But when Father Carey is poisoned, Donovan loses the will to live. On a respirator and locked inside his paralysed body there is nothing he can do about it. Or is there? Though unable to speak or move, there is nothing inactive about his mind. Can he find a way to track down the killer?

A BLOW TO THE HEART

Marcel Theroux

The violent death of Daisy's husband leaves her a widow in her early thirties. As she struggles to build a new life, a chance encounter with her husband's killer leads her on a journey into obsessive hatred. Daisy stalks the man, a small-time criminal and boxer called Joel Heath, and secretly pursues him into the twilight world of professional boxing. She befriends Tate, a boxing has-been, and his deaf protégé Isaac, in order to strike back at Heath. But Isaac's disability and his once-in-a-lifetime talent present Daisy with harder choices and more dangerous opponents than she could ever have imagined.